3 WILLOWS

the sisterhood grows

Books by
Ann Brashares

The Sisterhood of the Traveling Pants

The Second Summer of the Sisterhood

Girls in Pants: The Third Summer of the Sisterhood

Forever in Blue: The Fourth Summer of the Sisterhood

Please visit annbrashares.net for more about Ann

3 WILLOWS

the sisterhood grows

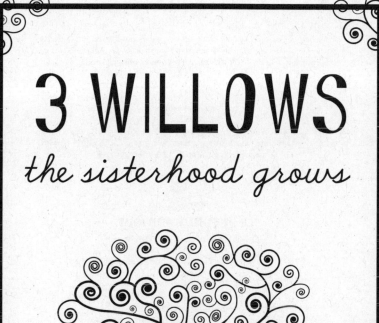

Ann Brashares

DELACORTE PRESS

Published by Delacorte Press
an imprint of Random House Children's Books
a division of Random House, Inc.
New York

Produced by Alloy Entertainment.

www.randomhouse.com/teens
www.sisterhoodcentral.com

Educators and librarians, for a variety of teaching tools,
visit us at www.randomhouse.com/teachers

Library of Congress Cataloging-in-Publication Data
Brashares, Ann.
3 willows : the sisterhood grows / Ann Brashares.—1st ed.
p. cm.
Summary: Ama, Jo, and Polly, three close friends from Bethesda, Maryland, spend the
summer before ninth grade learning about themselves, their families, and the changing
nature of their friendship.
ISBN 978-0-385-73676-3 (trade) — ISBN 978-0-385-90628-9 (lib. bdg.)
— ISBN 978-0-385-73813-2 (e-book)
[1. Best friends—Fiction. 2. Friendship—Fiction. 3. Interpersonal relations—Fiction.
4. Conduct of life—Fiction. 5. Bethesda (Md.)—Fiction.] I. Title.
II. Title: Three willows.
PZ7.B73759Aag 2009
[Fic]—dc22
2008034873

The text of this book is set in 12-point Cochin.

Book design by Marci Senders

Printed in the United States of America

10 9 8 7 6 5 4 3 2 1

First Edition

For Nancy Easton, with love
and gratitude for your friendship
through many children, many
books, and many miles.
Thanks for listening to my
thoughts about trees.

And for my beloved 3,
Sam, Nate, and Susannah.

Acknowledgments

I thank my steadfast editorial sisterhood once again:
Jennifer Rudolph Walsh, Beverly Horowitz, and
Wendy Loggia.

I thank my outstanding colleagues and friends at
Random House Children's Books: Chip Gibson,
Joan DeMayo, Marci Senders, Isabel Warren-Lynch,
Noreen Marchisi, Judith Haut, John Adamo,
Rachel Feld, and Tim Terhune.

As ever, I lovingly acknowledge my husband,
Jacob Collins, my children, Sam, Nate, and
Susannah, and my parents, Jane and Bill Brashares.

3 WILLOWS

the sisterhood grows

THE SMALLEST SPROUT SHOWS
THERE IS REALLY NO DEATH.

—WALT WHITMAN,
"SONG OF MYSELF"

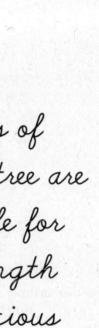

The roots of
the willow tree are
remarkable for
their strength
and tenacious
hold on life.

One

The last day of school was a half day. Tomorrow the entire eighth grade would pile back into the gym for the graduation ceremony, but that was just for an hour and their families would be there. The next time Ama went to school, it would be high school.

Everything is changing, Ama thought.

Usually she took the bus home, but today she felt like walking, she wasn't sure why. She wasn't sentimental. She was purposeful and forward-looking, like her older sister. But it was an aimless time of day, and she wasn't hauling her usual twenty pounds of textbooks, binders, and notebooks. Today she felt like treading the familiar steps she'd walked so many times when she was younger, when she was never in a hurry.

She couldn't help thinking about Polly and Jo as she walked, so when she saw them up ahead, waiting at the light to cross East-West Highway, it almost felt like they appeared out of her memory.

Ama was surprised to see Polly and Jo together. From this long view, she was struck by the naturalness of the way they stood together and at the same time, the strain. She doubted they had started off from school together. These days Jo usually left school with her noisy and flirting group of friends to go to the Tastee Diner or to the bagel place around the corner. Polly went her own way — taking forever to pack up her stuff and often spending time at the library before heading home. Ama sometimes saw Polly at the library and they sat together out of habit. But unlike Ama, Polly wasn't there to do her homework. Polly read everything in the library except what was assigned.

As Ama got closer, she considered how little Jo looked like she used to in elementary school. Her braces were off, her glasses were gone, and she devotedly wore whatever the current marker for popularity was — at the moment, pastel plaid shorts and her hair in two braids. Ama considered how much Polly, in her long frayed shorts and her dark newsboy cap, looked the same as she always had.

"Ama! Hey!" Polly saw her first. She was waving excitedly. The walk sign illuminated and Ama hurried to catch up to them so they could cross the highway together.

"I can't believe you're here," Polly said, looking from Ama to Jo. "This is historic."

"It's on her way home," Jo pointed out, not seeming to want to acknowledge the significance of the three of them walking home together on this day.

Ama understood how Jo felt. The history of their friendship was like a brimming and moody pond under a smooth surface of ice, and she didn't want to crack it.

As they walked they talked about final exams and graduation plans. Nobody said anything as they passed the 7-Eleven or even as they approached the old turn.

What if we turned? Ama suddenly wondered. What if they ran down the old hill, past the playground, and stepped into the woods to see the little trees they had planted so long ago? What if they held hands and ran as fast as they could?

But the three of them passed the old turn, heads and eyes forward. Only Polly seemed to glance back for a moment.

Anyway, even if they did turn, Ama knew it wouldn't be the same. The creaky metal merry-go-round would be rusted, the swing set abandoned. The trees might not even be there anymore. It had been so long since they'd tended to them.

Ama pictured her younger self, running down the hill with her two best friends, out of control and exhilarated.

It was different now. People changed and places changed. They were going into high school. This was no time for looking back. Ama couldn't even picture the trees. She couldn't remember the name of the hill anymore.

Polly

When I think of the first day of our friendship, I think of the three of us running across East-West Highway with our backpacks on our backs and our potted plants in our hands. I think of Jo dropping her plant in the middle of the street and all of us stopping short, and the sight of the little stalk turned on its side and the roots showing and the soil spilling onto the asphalt. I remember the three of us stooping down to put the plant back into its pot, hurriedly tucking its roots back under the dirt as the walk signal turned from white WALK to blinking orange DON'T WALK. And I remember Ama shouting that we had to hurry, and seeing, over my shoulder, the cars pouring over the hill toward us. I remember the rough feeling of the asphalt scraping under my fingers as I swept up the last of the dirt, the stinging feeling of my knuckles as I tried to gather it in my fist. I think it was Jo who grabbed my arm and pulled me to the sidewalk. And I remember the long, flat swell of the horns in my ears.

Ama

We met on the first day of third grade, because of all the 132 kids in our grade, we were the three who didn't get picked up. I was spooked, because my mom had never failed to pick me up from school. She'd never even been late before.

We didn't talk to each other at first. I was embarrassed and scared and I didn't want to show it. They put us in the math help room with the see-through walls. We stared out like a zoo exhibit waiting for our parents to come.

That was the day they gave out the little willow tree cuttings in plastic pots in our science class. We were supposed to take care of them and study them all year. I remember each of us sitting at a desk with our plant in front of us. Polly kept poking at hers to see if the soil was too dry. She hummed.

Jo put her sneakers up on the desk and leaned back. She said her plant probably wouldn't last through the week.

I couldn't believe how casual the two of them were about being left at school. I was freaked out, but later on I learned that my mother had a really good excuse for not showing up that day.

Jo

I guess it was my idea to run away from school together. We'd been waiting for like an hour and a half for our parents and we were bored and hungry. Me especially. They'd moved us to the chairs outside the principal's office, so we felt like we were getting punished. Ms. Lorenz, the principal's assistant, tried to track down our parents, while all the other teachers went home.

Ama had to go to the bathroom, so Polly and I went with her. We started poking around in empty classrooms and stood on the tables in the cafeteria. It was kind of fun being in school when it was empty and the lights were off. As we walked past the back doors I dared Ama and Polly to walk out of them, and to my shock they did. So there we were, standing outside the school. We hadn't meant to leave, but once we had, I just couldn't go back in there. Freedom's a one-way street, and we were already on it.

"Let's go," I said. It felt like summer and I knew the way home.

Ama was the one who hesitated.

"We'll get you home," Polly promised her.

We ran through the backstreets to the 7-Eleven. I had a twenty-dollar bill in my backpack for emergencies, so we gorged on blue Slurpees and Cheetos and Butterfingers. Then it started to rain, to really pour, so we sat in the front window and watched the steam

9

rising in the parking lot and the sky darken practically to night. We wanted to play Dragon Slayer, the old arcade game they had there, but it had yellow tape strung across the front.

The air was cool and sparkling when we left. We ran home across East-West Highway. I remember running with our plants. A plant is one of the few things you can't stuff into your backpack. I remember my little stalk swaying and trembling as I ran. We nearly got killed when I dropped it in the middle of the street.

We took Ama home first. We walked to her building and up to her apartment, where her father was frantically calling school. That's when we found out about her brother, Bob, who was born that afternoon.

On the way to Polly's she was doing that little skip-step she does when she's happy. We went up to her door and she said her mom wasn't home but that was okay. She said her mom always lost track of time when she was working in her studio. I saw Dia's sculptures for the first time on the front porch—big bare winter trees made out of broken wristwatches and old cell phones. We went around back and I watched Polly expertly push open a window and climb through it, like that was the regular way into her house.

"I never had a friend take me home," she said to me through the open window.

Polly

There are moments in your life when the big pieces slide and shift. Sometimes the big changes don't happen gradually but all at once. That's how it was for us. That was the day we discovered that friends can do things for you that your parents can't.

On the bus ride home from Grace's house two days after the end of school, Ama felt shaky with nervous excitement. Her dad had called her on her cell phone, telling her that the letter had finally arrived. He'd offered to pick her up on his way home, but she knew he'd show up in his taxicab, so she opted for the bus. It wasn't that she was ashamed of his driving a cab. That wasn't it. She just didn't like people trying to flag them down as they drove by. She wanted them to be able to drive along in privacy like a regular family and not like they were for hire. And her dad was really nice, so if it was someone old or disabled hailing them down, he would usually stop, even if he was off duty, and sometimes he wouldn't make them pay anything.

To her parents' great pleasure, Ama had won a summer study grant from the Student Leader Foundation, which meant her entire summer was paid for, including travel. It was a big honor. Only two hundred students across the country got the grants, and nobody in her school had gotten one since her sister, Esi. Esi had won the grant four years in a row.

Now it was just a question of which program Ama would get into. Ama's first choice was the summer school at Andover, where her friend Grace was going. That was a very popular first choice, she knew, so she probably wouldn't get it. Her second choice was working for school credit at an office of Habitat for Humanity in Virginia. That would look good on her transcript—at least, that was what Esi told her. Her third choice was an academic camp run by Johns Hopkins University in Baltimore.

Her five-year-old brother, Bob, was standing at the door, flapping the fat envelope, when she walked in. Her parents joined them in the hallway. "I will guess it's Hopkins," her mother pronounced.

Ama sometimes felt self-conscious about how involved her parents—and even her brother—became in her academic life. Jo used to joke that her mom didn't know her homeroom teacher's name and her dad didn't know what grade she was in.

"That's because the Napolis are rich," Ama's mother said to her once. "They don't need to care as much as we do."

"I guess it's Habitat," her dad said.

"Can I open it?" Bob shouted.

"I told you, you have to let Ama open it," her mother scolded.

"You can open it," Ama said to Bob. Bob had an irrational

12

love of opening mail, and he almost never got any. "Just don't rip it."

Bob nodded seriously. He opened it with great care, handing the pages to her one at a time. Ama's heart was speeding and her eyes were flying around for the part that mattered.

She studied one page and then the next and the third.

"Which one is it?" her mother prodded.

"I don't see it. I think it's — " Ama turned one of the papers over. "It's . . . I don't get it. It says Wild Adventures." In vain she scanned for words like *Andover* or *Johns Hopkins*.

Her mother looked doubtful. "Let me see."

"The address is in Wyoming. It looks like some kind of outdoors trip." Ama went back to the first page. "They must have made a mistake. I didn't sign up for that."

"Wild Adventures?" her father said.

"That's a mistake. Hold on." Ama tried to locate her name to make sure she hadn't gotten somebody else's assignment. No, it did have her name and address right.

Bob was continuing to pull papers out of the envelope. One of them fluttered to the floor. Ama's mom picked it up. "This is an airline ticket," her mom said in wonderment. "To Jackson, Wyoming."

"A plane ticket?"

"This says money!" Bob proclaimed excitedly, flapping yet another item.

"Hold on," Ama said, grabbing it from Bob. It did say money. It was a check for $288. It said "equipment stipend" on the stub. It came from the Student Leader Foundation and was made out directly to her. "They sent me money?" She didn't even have a bank account yet.

"Let me look," her father said.

"Can I have a dollar?" Bob asked.

"No. Wait. Hang on." Ama was getting that overwhelmed feeling, and she really hated it. She gathered up all the papers and put them in order. She read them carefully, passing each sheet to her father when she was done with it. *Yosemite, the Grand Tetons, Wind Cave, the Badlands.* The Badlands? What kind of program was this?

Bob had by this point moved on to bending a paper clip that had fallen off the papers.

"It looks like they messed this up," Ama finally declared. "It looks like they gave me a scholarship to this outdoor trip where they have you hike and climb mountains in national parks." She looked at her parents. She shook her head as though the foundation had mistakenly sent her a pet skunk. "This is all wrong. I'm not going to do it."

Ama

Our plants did survive third grade. Even Jo's. She tried to act like she couldn't be bothered to take care of it, but I could tell she could. I spent a lot of time at her house with her and Polly that year, even

14

though my parents disapproved of going to friends' houses when you had homework. My sister, Esi, never did that, they reminded me. So I know Jo played her violin to her plant and even got it some special food.

The plants magically turned from cuttings to actual tiny trees, and the roots grew and wound all up. There was barely enough soil in the pots anymore, so we had to put them in bigger pots. You had to water them practically every day.

Polly had the idea of planting them on the last day of school. She found the perfect spot in a little woods with a creek behind a playground at the end of my street. It was the woods at the bottom of Pony Hill, the best sledding hill in the world, where we used to play a lot. There was a clearing where we planted all three in a row with enough space between them to grow deep roots. We dug with our fingers because we forgot to bring a trowel. We pulled out the rocks and tried not to disturb the worms too much because Polly insisted we needed their help. We carefully undid the root balls. It was like untangling hair. We tucked them into the dirt.

It was weird taking the plants from the tiny world of soil in their pots and putting them into the ground, connected to all the other things in the earth. They looked kind of shy and vulnerable, and it was hard to leave them. They didn't seem like they belonged there. Jo looked like she was going to cry when we walked away.

We checked on them a lot that first summer. Jo often brought her violin and the plant food. And in fourth grade, we met up almost every day after school. Sometimes we got Slurpees and candy bars at the 7-Eleven and checked on our trees on the way home.

15

Two

Polly

Jo was really good at violin back then. She practiced with her dad, who also played, but she quickly got better than him. He was really proud of her and said she could be a professional if she worked hard.

She could play along with Top Forty songs on the radio. Even rap songs, which was really hilarious. She could figure out almost any tune. She played so loud she could blow your ears out.

Jo

For some reason, Dia, Polly's mom, got a tattoo when we were in fourth grade. It was a spiderweb that went all around her belly *button. I thought it was very cool. I thought it would be awesome to have a mom with a tattoo.*

Polly slept over my house that night, and when we were falling asleep she was crying and said she wished her mom hadn't gotten it. I couldn't understand that at the time, but as I get older I think I do.

Jo hoisted her duffel bag onto the pile of her stuff accumulating in the front hall. Her mother's suitcases were lined up in the corner, neatly topped by a couple of sun hats and several shoe boxes. They weren't leaving until the next day, but it was a big job to pack for the whole summer.

Her mother drifted into the hall to survey the progress. "Jo, what's with all this junk? I wish you'd clean it up. Do you really need your skateboard?"

"It's not junk. It's my stuff. Anyway, we're just going to pack it in the car," Jo said. Her mom did not like messes or disorder of any kind. Not even the temporary messes that were unavoidable when packing or moving.

"Where's Dad's stuff? Where are his golf clubs?"

Her mom plucked a straw sun hat from atop her suitcase and began restoring its shape.

"Mom?"

"I guess he'll bring it when he comes out," she said.

"When's that? I thought he was coming with us."

Jo's mom lowered the hat and looked at her. "He's not."

"Why not? Is he on call?"

"Yes."

"All summer?"

"Jo, please."

Her mom didn't want to talk about it, and that made Jo need to talk about it.

"So when's he coming, then?"

"Why don't you ask him yourself?"

"Why, because you two can't talk to each other?"

Her mom averted her eyes even more quickly than Jo expected her to. Her voice got quieter. "You should discuss it with your dad."

Jo tried to remember when exactly it was that her mom had stopped calling him "Dad" when she spoke of him to Jo and started calling him "your dad."

"Really, you should talk to him before we go. You should ask him about his plans," her mom said again.

What's that supposed to mean? What are you trying to tell me? Jo wanted to say, but she closed her mouth. Was torturing her mother really worth torturing herself? Did she really want to know?

"I can talk to him when he gets to the beach," Jo said blithely, turning away and running up the stairs. "I can talk to him all summer."

• • •

Jo

Ama's sister, Esi, got into Princeton when Ama and Polly and I were in fourth grade, and she went there the next year. That's a big reason the family moved to the United States from Ghana in the first place. They wanted Esi to go to the best possible college without having to send her across the world from them. So it was a really big deal when Esi got in, and her family had a celebration and everything. Ama's mom is an incredible cook. I should know, because I ate dinner there almost every night in fifth grade and even probably a lot of sixth grade too. My dad was working a lot then, and my mom wasn't in much of a mood to cook.

Esi started college when she was sixteen, because she skipped two grades. You'd think that would take the pressure off Ama a little, having her genius sister gone, but if anything that made it worse.

Polly

Jo's older brother was Finn. He had wavy hair and turquoise eyes. He tried to teach us how to skateboard. He died at the end of the summer, right before fifth grade. He was going to be in eighth grade.

Finn had a problem with his heart. Two times before he died he'd blacked out. Once when he was ten and the second time at the beginning of the school year when he was twelve—the same time Jo and Ama and I met. He'd gone to the hospital, and they'd done a bunch

19

of tests but hadn't figured out what was wrong. It didn't seem like a big deal back then.

The week he died is a blur to me, but I remember the burial. Jo left before it was over. She was supposed to pour a shovelful of dirt on the coffin after her parents, but instead she put the shovel down and just walked away. Ama and I followed her. We sat on the hood of her uncle's car in the parking lot, throwing pebbles at a metal sign. I can still hear the clink clink clink of the stones when they hit.

It was really lucky that the three of us were in the same classroom that year, because Ama and I could stay close to Jo. She didn't talk about it and we didn't ask her anything. We were her friends; we knew what to say and it seemed like nobody else did. I felt like we made a wall around her. That was what she needed us to do.

We knew how it was at Jo's house, so the three of us spent most afternoons and a lot of weekends at Ama's, even though Ama's parents made us do our homeowrk all the time. I never got so many As as in fifth grade.

Ama promised she wouldn't skip any grades because she wanted to stay with us.

Jo stopped playing the violin because she said it was too loud.

Two or three times a year Polly went to visit her uncle Hoppy at the old-age home a mile from her house. Sometimes when he felt spry, they walked to the diner around the corner and ordered soup.

Hoppy might not have been her uncle. She wasn't

20

precisely sure what he was. But he was some kind of much older relative on her dad's side—the only relative she'd ever met on her dad's side—so it seemed important to stay in touch. Hoppy might have been her great-great-uncle or her third cousin five times removed. He was very hazy about the family tree, and Polly didn't want to press him too hard on it. It was just nice to think there was someone.

That was why when other kids were packing up and heading off to camp or to the beach, Polly was sitting in a red Naugahyde booth in a greasy-spoon diner across from a very old man with hair fluffing out his ears.

The two bowls of chicken noodle soup arrived, and Polly held up her spoon. "Hey," she said. "They really do have greasy spoons here."

"What's that?" Uncle Hoppy's face creased up on one side and he leaned toward her.

"My spoon is actually greasy," Polly said buoyantly. She didn't want to say it too loudly in case she hurt the employees' feelings.

"Your spoon?" he barked. "Your spoon is what? Do you need a new spoon?"

Polly put it down. "No, it's fine." She wondered if the ear hair was getting in the way of Uncle Hoppy's hearing.

"How's your mother?"

"Very well, thanks."

"She still making those . . . ?" Hoppy cocked his head like a Labrador. "What are those things she makes?"

"Sculptures."

"What's that?" Hoppy put his hand to his ear.

"Sculptures! Yes. She still makes them." Polly nodded broadly to help with the hearing problem.

"Very pretty girl, your mother," Hoppy said.

Polly's mother had spiky black hair and a pierced nose, but Polly didn't argue.

"You too." He sized Polly up through squinting, cloudy eyes. "You're a very pretty girl."

"Thank you," Polly said. She didn't put huge faith in his eyesight, based on the amount of help he needed with the menu.

"Very pretty. You could be a model."

Polly laughed. "You think so?"

"Yes. Your grandmother was a model, you know." He bobbed his head at the memory. "Now, there was a very pretty girl."

Polly swallowed her mouthful of soup without chewing the noodles. "My grandmother?" Those were normal words to most people but startling words to her. She'd never had a grandmother. Dia hadn't spoken to her mother since she left home at seventeen. "I don't know if she's alive or dead and I don't really care" was pretty much all Dia had ever said about her mother. Polly had never heard a word spoken of her father's mother. She forgot that there had to have been such a person.

"She was a looker, all right." Hoppy waggled his eyebrows suggestively. He was just too old to be really offensive. "Your grandmother looked like Sophia Loren. You probably don't know who that is."

"Yes I do," Polly said with a touch of pride. Polly knew her movie stars, especially the old ones. In fact, his words struck Polly. Of all the truly beautiful and glamorous movie stars, the only one Polly had ever secretly believed she resembled was Sophia Loren. And also maybe Penélope Cruz a tiny, tiny bit.

"You look like your grandmother," Hoppy pronounced. "Like a model."

Polly was fascinated. She wished Hoppy could hear better. "You mean she was, like, a professional model? Like in magazines?" she nearly shouted at him.

"What's that?"

"Was she in *magazines*? Do you have any *pictures*?"

Hoppy knocked his bowl around in its saucer. "Yes. All the magazines. She was in all of them."

"Really? Do you *have any pictures of her*?"

"Do I have them? No. I don't think I have them. That was a long time ago."

Polly nodded, her mind flying, her heart swelling. She had a grandmother and her grandmother had been a model. She had a grandmother who was beautiful and she looked like Sophia Loren.

Polly watched as though from a distance, a floating perch near the ceiling, as Uncle Hoppy wrestled with the bill and means of payment. It became such a confusion that Polly eventually had to come down from her reveries on the ceiling and settle it herself with her own ten-dollar bill.

She walked with Hoppy around the corner to his senior residence, bouncing along beside him. She knew with the traffic rushing along Wisconsin Avenue he wouldn't hear a word she said, so she didn't try.

A part of her was burning to ask him whether this grandmother was still alive, and how her life had gone, and what her name was. But another part of Polly was content to stay dreamily quiet.

This knowledge was a gift, shimmering like a cloud in front of her eyes. She was afraid that if she tried to hold it in her hands she would be left, again, owning nothing.

Mrs. Sherman, assistant director of the Student Leader Foundation, was admirably patient with Ama on the phone when Ama finally reached her a few hours later. Almost too patient.

"Ama, as I said, this is not an error. This is your placement. It's an excellent scholarship. In fact, it's one of the most valuable we offer."

"But it's not valuable to me. I don't really like the outdoors. I'm not outdoorsy. I'm more . . . indoorsy. I really didn't—this really isn't what I was hoping for."

Mrs. Sherman sighed for about the forty-fifth time. "Ama, not everyone gets one of their top choices. Our committee members think long and hard about what will be the best fit for our leadership scholars."

"But this is not the best fit," Ama said imploringly. "This is the *worst* fit. Anyone who knows me knows that."

"Ama, maybe you can keep an open mind about this. I hope you'll realize that it represents a once-in-a-lifetime opportunity."

Ama couldn't keep an open mind. She didn't have an open mind. She didn't even want an open mind. She wanted Andover! She wanted books and libraries and classes where she could get good grades! She wanted A-pluses and gold stars and extra credit.

"I need credit," Ama said, trying to sound practical. "I need a program that gives high school credit."

"Oh, this gives credit," Mrs. Sherman said triumphantly. "It gives full course credit. Read the description. You'll see."

Ama felt herself shriveling and shrinking. She hated being wrong, and she hated being wrong on account of poor preparation even more. "Oh . . . really?" Ama said quietly.

"Ama, I know it's not what you wanted, but it's a fantastic program. One of our best. I know it doesn't seem like it to you now, but you are very fortunate to get it. . . ."

Ama stopped listening. She just waited for Mrs. Sherman to finish. "But do you think, for personal reasons, I could change it?" Ama asked finally.

"Not without a valid medical condition. Of course, you could forfeit the scholarship altogether."

No she couldn't! This scholarship was a big prize. It would go on her school record. Colleges would see it. She couldn't forfeit it. Anyway, her parents would never let her.

"Do you have a valid medical reason?" Mrs. Sherman asked.

I'm scared of heights. I hate bugs. I can't live without my flatiron and my hair products. Were any of those valid medical conditions?

"I don't know. I'll have to think about it," Ama said defeatedly.

Ama tried to be polite with her good-byes and thank-yous. She hung up the phone and went to find her mother. "The woman from the Student Leader office says it's not a mistake."

"I know you're disappointed, *chérie*," her mother said.

Ama cast her eye on the check clipped to the front of her papers. She'd never gotten that kind of money before. Miserably she looked over the long equipment list. She couldn't believe she was going to spend the only easy money she'd ever gotten in her life on hiking boots and a sleeping bag, wool pants, and something called a carabiner.

I don't want to go, I don't want to go, I don't want to go. "I guess I have to go" was what Ama said out loud.

She looked at her mother, irrationally hoping that she would disagree and grab the phone and make calls and demand changes on her daughter's behalf.

But her mother didn't. Her parents trusted the system. It had done well for Esi and it would do well for Ama. "You're a good girl, Ama."

Ama nodded, both happy and unhappy, as she often was with that reward.

Three

Ama

    We first heard about the Sisterhood in sixth grade. You've probably never heard of them, but they became, like, a legend around here. They were four girls who went to our local high school and they shared a pair of jeans that were supposed to be, like, magical. The jeans fit all four of them, and the girls passed them around and decorated them and wrote all over them. These girls had been really, really close friends since they were babies. I haven't seen any of them—or the pants—except in the yearbook, but Jo knows Bridget Vreeland, and Polly sometimes babysits for Tibby Rollins's younger sister and brother. By now the Sisterhood has graduated and gone to college, but people still talk about them. They don't even seem real to me anymore. More like a story.

A lot of girls in our school tried to follow in their footsteps. It's the best reason I can give for a lot of terrible-fitting jeans in our middle school. Not every pair of jeans can fit a bunch of different girls. And I say that because I know. We tried it too. It's pretty embarrassing when I think of myself wearing Polly's jeans in sixth grade. This obnoxious boy shouted in the stairwell that I had plumber's crack, and some boys called me Plumber for months after that.

After the jeans, we tried to share a denim skirt, but I had a growth spurt, and it got so short on me that my mom wouldn't let me leave the apartment in it. We had a jean jacket for a while, but Polly accidentally left it on the boardwalk when we were visiting Jo at Rehoboth Beach. Then we got a scarf—green and blue and purple—at the beginning of seventh grade. We had an induction ceremony with candles and everything, but none of us really wore it much because . . . because a scarf is just pretty lame when you think about it.

Jo

Bridget Vreeland is one of the four girls of the Sisterhood. She was a coach at my soccer camp after sixth grade. She is basically the coolest girl you have ever seen. All the girls in my cabin thought that. Not just because she is gorgeous and an All-American soccer player and she hooked up with the hottest guy at our camp. But also because she has these awesome friends and the Traveling Pants. I actually saw her wearing them once. I think she's one of those people who's just lucky. Like she never had a problem or a zit or a bad day ever. That's how it seems to me.

The girls in my cabin used to follow her around, and one time we even caught her making out with Eric Richman at the lake. We thought it was unbelievably romantic. We were all giggling behind the bushes. She probably thought we were such little dorks.

I had the idea that being a teenager would be like that. That was how I imagined it could be for me and Polly and Ama when we got older. But you look at Polly, with her skipping and her weird doodles and sucking her thumb until she was in junior high. You can't really imagine her going to parties or having a boyfriend no matter how old she gets. You look at Ama now that she's a teenager. She won't even go to a movie with you because she has to do the extra-credit math problems. You can't imagine her having any big adventures. You can't even picture her going outside. When I think about the Sisterhood, I admit I kind of wish we were more like that.

I've seen Bridget in Bethesda a few times. I waved to her, but I don't think she remembers me. There were a lot of campers to keep track of.

Polly

Maybe we tried so hard to be like the Sisterhood because it was easy for them and we wanted it to be easy for us. Because they were lucky and we wanted to be lucky too. They had wonder, and we didn't have any.

We looked for the magic, but we didn't find it. We waited for the magic, but it didn't find us.

"Hey, Jo. It's Ama."

"Hey. What's up?"

Jo meant for her to answer the question, and Ama was silent for a second. It used to be that when she called Jo, Jo didn't expect her to have a reason right away.

"I'm packing to go on my trip. The list says I'm supposed to have a bandana. Remember that pink one I had? I think you borrowed it."

She heard Jo thumping around her room. "Oh, yeah. I did. That was a while ago." Jo was opening and closing drawers. "Yeah. I have it. Do you want me to bring it over?"

"Or I could pick it up if you want."

"No, I'll bring it over."

"Also, do you have those blue wool socks with the stars? I think I lent them to you when you went skiing, like, last year."

"Hang on." Jo put the phone down and then came back. "I don't see them. I think Polly has those."

"Okay, thanks. I'll call Polly."

When Ama called Polly, Polly said she couldn't find the socks right away, but she promised she'd look around and bring them over if she found them.

Ama was dutifully, somewhat miserably, oiling her boots later when she heard the door.

Her mom got to it first. She kissed Jo on both cheeks and hugged her hard. "Look at you! How long since I've seen you? Look at your hair so long! You got your braces off?"

"Mom, she got her braces off like a year ago," Ama said flatly.

"Well. She looks so grown."

Ama was embarrassed by her mom's exuberance, but Jo didn't seem to mind.

"Are you staying for dinner? It's Ama's going-away dinner. I'm making kyinkyinga. That's the kind of kebab you love."

Jo smiled and glanced at Ama a little awkwardly. "I—no, I . . . I can't really stay. I'm supposed to . . ." Her voice trailed off.

"Mama, Jo has stuff to do," Ama jumped in. "She's going away too." She signaled to Jo to follow her to her room. She noticed that Jo was carrying a box.

Jo put it down when the doorbell rang again. This time Ama sprinted to make sure she got there first. It was Polly, carrying a brown paper grocery bag in one hand and Ama's socks in the other.

"I found them," Polly declared.

"Hey, thanks," Ama said. "Thanks for bringing them over." She led Polly back to her room. "Jo is here," she said on the way. She kept her voice even, not registering that it was unusual to have both Jo and Polly in her apartment, not even noticing that the three of them hadn't been together there since her family's annual Easter dinner.

"She is?"

Ama pushed open the door to her room and there, indeed, was Jo.

Jo looked a little surprised and a little suspicious, like maybe she'd been set up.

"Polly did have the socks," Ama explained.

"Oh, right," Jo said.

Polly held up the socks. The three of them stared at each other for a minute.

"What's in the box?" Ama asked Jo.

Jo looked into her box. "I figured I'd return your other stuff," she said. "Since I was bringing the bandana." She took out a pile of DVDs, a few bangle bracelets, some books, and a T-shirt.

"You didn't have to bring all that," Ama said. She looked at the DVDs. "You love *The Princess Bride*. I said you could keep that."

Jo shrugged. "I doubt I'm going to watch it again. Maybe Bob's old enough for it."

Polly, too, had brought more than just Ama's socks: a mix CD, a hooded sweatshirt, and a pile of Beanie Babies—a chick, a lobster, a fish, a moose, and two bears.

"Polly, you seriously do not need to return those," Ama said, shaking her head at the pile.

"I know, but I just figured . . ."

Ama wasn't sure what to say. There was too much to say to say anything. She turned to her closet. "Okay, well . . . I guess I should give you your stuff back too." In her closet she found two of Jo's shirts. On her bookshelf she found all of Polly's Little House and Anne of Green Gables books. She'd had them since fourth grade.

"I'm sure there's more," Ama said.

Jo sat on her bed and Polly sat on her floor as she criss-crossed her room, making piles for each of them.

"Dinner will be ready in fifteen minutes," Ama's mother called. Those were the only words in the room. Ama heard her dad's voice faintly from the kitchen.

Ama finished the piles, and Jo and Polly boxed and bagged them.

"You guys can stay for dinner. If you want." As Ama said it, she wasn't sure what she wanted.

Jo picked up her box, fuller than it was when she brought it. "I can't. I'm meeting Bryn and Kylie and Marie and those guys for pizza."

Jo didn't issue any invitations, and Ama didn't expect one. She wasn't friends with that crowd, and Polly certainly wasn't either.

Ama looked at Polly. Polly looked uncertain. "Is it just your family?"

"Grace is coming too." Grace was Ama's lab partner and the only other kid in their grade who'd been invited to take the SAT in middle school.

"I should probably get home," Polly said softly.

Ama walked them to the door and they said good-bye. They said things that friends would say, that they partly meant.

Have a great trip. Write me. Call when you get back. Tell so-and-so hi.

Jo said maybe she'd see them at the beach. In past summers Ama and Polly had always gone to visit for some part of it, but she must have known this year they probably wouldn't.

Ama watched Jo and Polly troop down the hallway to the elevator, carrying their stuff. All their possessions were finally restored to rightful ownership. Under that fact was the nag of the feeling. What little they'd still had of each other they didn't have anymore.

Jo

When did we last visit the willow trees? I don't even know. I might have stopped first. Polly and Ama might have kept going. No, I'm pretty sure Ama stopped too. She doesn't do things for no reason anymore. Polly might have kept going, but I don't know.

The seeds of the willow
are carried by long,
silky white strands and
widely dispersed on
the wind.

Four

Jo's bedroom at the beach was painted the same shade of blue-green as her bedroom at home. It had a slightly tattered quilt left over from her grandmother in Kentucky and some second-string furniture brought from the house in Bethesda. She had jars of sea glass along her windowsills, glinting colors both rare and ordinary. She liked this room. She liked the degree of worn-ness that wasn't really permitted at home.

In the past they'd mostly used this house for weekends and short vacations, and in the old days Jo had often brought Ama and Polly along. Jo knew her family was different from most of the other beach families in that way. Most moms brought their kids out for the whole summer while the dads commuted on weekends. But after Finn, Jo started going to sleep-away camp for summers, and her parents never came here when it was just the two of them. The Napolis had one of the biggest houses on the beach and used it least, and Jo guessed that did not endear them to the community.

"Who are we keeping this place for?" she had once overheard her dad ask her mom.

"For the kids," her mom had said. "For Jo," she corrected herself.

This summer Jo would have happily gone back to her sleep-away soccer camp in Pennsylvania. She had loved it, but this summer she was too old to be a camper and too young to be a counselor. Both she and her mom were set off balance at the idea of her being home for the summer again. That was how the idea of spending the summer at the beach house had come up. There were several kids Jo knew here, including her friend Bryn from school. Bryn was part of the group Jo had begun to hang out with in seventh grade. Bryn wasn't the greatest listener, but she was loyal, and just being her friend put you at the center of the action. Bryn had told Jo there were a lot of kids from their high school who came for the summer and got jobs on the boardwalk. And Bryn was the one who'd told her about the bus girl job at the Surfside. She said it was one of the few jobs you could get when you were fourteen.

In the beginning Jo thought it was her idea to spend the summer at the beach, but later she wondered if her parents had thought of it already.

Jo finished putting her things away in her drawers. Before now, her dresser had seemed like a sizable prop—like the dressers in hotels where you never actually put your stuff. This was her bedroom, but she'd never been here long enough to pack very much or really bother to settle in. This time she would. This time she would get bored in this room; she would have beach friends over, she would talk on the phone, she would sit on the floor, she would scuff up the walls, Scotch-tape random quotations and pictures on them. She would fill up the garbage can and leave dirty socks around. She would keep her door closed to shield her mom from the mess.

It was getting to be dinnertime, and Jo didn't want to stay and eat dinner with just her mom. If her dad had been there, she wouldn't have wanted to eat dinner with just him and her mom either, because the two of them would fight or be silent. She didn't want to eat dinner with any combination of them, and she didn't want to eat dinner by herself. She pictured herself in a room full of strangers.

"I'm going to check on my application at the Surfside," she called to her mother as she walked toward the front door.

"I thought you were supposed to wait for them to contact

you," her mother said from the kitchen, where she was Windexing the glass fronts of the cabinets. Practically the entire house was made of glass, and her mother hated smudges and fingerprints.

"Well, now they won't have to," Jo said.

"Oh, I forgot to tell you," her mom shouted after her. "Polly called."

"She did? Did she leave a message?"

"Just that she called."

"All right," Jo said over her shoulder, and shut the door behind her. Jo hadn't checked her cell phone, but Polly had probably called that, too.

Jo walked onto the beach from Oak Avenue. She took off her shoes and walked along the water until she got to the northern part of the boardwalk where the restaurant sat. It was a big seasonal crab house, popular with vacationers and day-trippers alike. Most of the walls were sliding glass, so you could open them up to the ocean breeze. Tables were picnic style, with metal boxes of Old Bay seasoning and rolls of paper towels every few feet.

She had loved this place when she was younger. She remembered the sting of the seasoning on her fingers and the texture of the powdery pastel mints with the gumdrop center kept in a bowl by the door. She would often grab the outlaw second handful of mints on the way out. The first handful tasted good and the second tasted like guilt. She had once confessed it to Father Stickel first thing after her Act of Contrition. He was so good at taking her junior crimes seriously.

As a family, they never really went to the Surfside anymore. "Too touristy," her mom said. Jo didn't understand the big problem with tourists. Jo liked them. She often felt like one of them, even at home.

The dinner hour had not yet begun, so she walked straight to the back office. The door was open and the assistant manager was playing solitaire on the computer.

"I came to check on my application," she said.

He had longish hair and a lot of pimples, and though she could tell he was tall even sitting down, she could also tell he weighed about as much as she did, which was not all that much.

"I'm Jo Napoli. I'm a friend of Bryn's. She's starting this week."

"How old are you?" he asked. He tried to sound suspicious and authoritative, but his voice cracked in the middle of it.

How old are you? she felt like asking him back, but she stifled it. "Fourteen." She cleared her throat in a mature fashion. "And a half," she added, and then cursed herself for it. What a terrible touch. Who over the age of six ever added the half?

It gave him the upper hand. His pimples seemed to

recede. He clicked off his solitaire game. "I'll check your Social Security number," he said, hands poised over keyboard.

"It's on my application," she said, trying to look large. She ran her fingers through her hair, which seemed to make him nervous again.

"*Jo*, you said?" He riffled through a stack of papers. "Your name is Jo? As in Joseph?"

"As in Jo."

"Are you a female?"

She rolled her eyes.

He tried another stack of papers.

"Okay, here you go," he said, pulling one out. He studied it for a moment. "It looks like you're hired."

"I am?"

"I wouldn't have hired you, but I guess somebody did."

"Gee. Thanks."

"You're supposed to start tomorrow. You're a busboy."

"Bus girl."

He brought his solitaire game back to life. "Whatever."

Polly had heated up the leftover spaghetti and meatballs from when she and Dia had gone out to dinner on Sunday night. Polly sat at the little kitchen table, staring at her full plate and trying not to eat it. Her mother's share was still in the pot because she was staying late at her studio again.

Polly wound up a forkful of noodles and considered them. Models didn't eat spaghetti and meatballs, did they? They mostly ate salads, she suspected. Maybe she could start making salads for her and Dia. If they didn't involve blue cheese dressing or olives of any kind, then maybe Polly could get herself to like them.

Later that night, lying in her bed, Polly couldn't enjoy *Little Women* because her stomach was grumbling and her brain kept abandoning the March girls and jumping instead to thoughts of the Girl Scout cookies in the pantry. She'd bought them from Sasha Thomas, one of the girls she regularly babysat. In fact, Polly had ended up spending all the money she got from babysitting Sasha on Sasha's cookies, because Sasha was hoping to win an award from her troop for most cookie sales.

Polly finally padded down to the kitchen in her nightgown and ate four Samoas, seven Thin Mints, three Do-si-dos, and one Tagalong, and then she felt like she was going to barf. That was not model behavior, was it? Well, not unless she actually barfed on purpose. Maybe she should have just eaten her spaghetti at dinnertime.

Polly wanted so much to talk about her grandmother. She wanted her mom to come home so she could ask if her mom had ever met her grandmother, if she knew anything about her or maybe even had a picture she could show Polly. Some nights Polly didn't mind so much when her mom came home late and just went right upstairs and fell into bed, but other nights, like this one, she hated it. She had so many questions lined up, she'd actually written some of them down.

Polly checked the time. Nine o'clock wasn't too late. She wanted to call Jo, but she had called Jo two nights ago and Jo hadn't called back yet. She dialed Jo's number anyway. First the cell, and when Jo didn't answer, the phone at the beach house. She couldn't help it.

"Hello?" Jo's mom answered.

"Hi, Judy, it's Polly. Again. Is Jo there?"

"Hi, hon. No, she's out with some friends. I'll tell her you called."

Judy sounded sad to her. Polly hoped she wasn't sad that Polly was calling too much.

"Did she get a job?" Polly asked. It seemed sort of pathetic to be getting information about Jo through Jo's mother.

"Yes, at the Surfside. As a bus girl. She's starting tomorrow."

"That's great," Polly said. For half a second she was tempted to tell Judy about her grandmother, but she stopped herself. She wasn't that pathetic.

Ama stood at the gate in Jackson, Wyoming, in bewilderment. It had been a long and strange day—the third time she'd been on an airplane in her life and the first time alone. It was strange to be going all this way from home only to meet strangers.

She wondered whom she would first see from her group. She wondered what they would look like and whether they would recognize her. She wondered, did they have her picture? Did they know she was black? If so, she would not be tricky to spot in this place. She was the only nonwhite person in the whole airport, from what she could tell. Did they even have black people in Wyoming?

Her sister had gone so many places on her own that Ama felt she had no right to make a big deal of it, even to herself. Esi had flown to China for the International Mathematical Olympiad when she was thirteen. She'd been to math competitions in Berlin and Kazakhstan by the time she was fifteen, and when she was sixteen she'd moved from home into her dorm room at Princeton.

Ama spent her worry on wondering what to do about the things in her bag. She knew the trip leaders would do an equipment check right away, and she didn't want to bring suspicion upon herself.

"Ama? Are you Ama Botsio?"

It was a nice-looking twenty-something-year-old guy wearing a T-shirt that said GO WILD! He had sporty sunglasses dangling from a cord around his neck.

"Yes," she said, swallowing the word as she said it.

He stuck out his hand and shook hers. She felt the bones in her hand being crushed. She couldn't even get through a firm handshake. How was she going to climb up rocks?

"Nice to meet you," he said. "I'm Jared. I'm one of your group leaders."

"You too," she mumbled. She gingerly moved her fingers around, trying to reconstruct them.

"You're the last flight to arrive," he said, leading her down the corridor. "The rest of the group is out in the parking lot."

She expected him to notice that she was staggering under the weight of her gear and offer to help, but he didn't. He sailed along at a rapid pace, holding nothing but a clipboard.

I will be defeated by the walk through the airport, she thought miserably, watching him get farther and farther ahead.

Out in the mostly empty parking lot there were a bunch of kids milling around a long collapsible table set up in front of a bus. It wasn't a fancy air-conditioned bus with tinted windows and plush seats where they played movies. It was an old yellow school bus.

Ama was sweating under the weight of her pack as they approached. She wished she had an extra hand to pat her hair and make sure it was behaving before she met all these people.

Ama had always felt she had the Jekyll and Hyde of hair.

When it was conditioned and ironed and the weather wasn't too humid, she loved her hair. It hung like a smooth and shiny curtain, envied by even her sister. When Ama's hair was being good, she liked almost everything about how she looked. But when it wasn't properly conditioned or ironed or the weather was bad, it started to frizz and puff. It started to pile up and defy gravity in a terrible way. The longer she left it, the worse it got. And when her hair was being evil, Ama thought every part of her was ugly. Her eyes didn't get smaller and her neck didn't get skinnier and her ears didn't stick out more just because her hair was behaving badly, but that was how it felt to her.

She surveyed the color array of her group and found it nearly all white. There was an Asian girl. She wouldn't suffer over her hair. There was a kid who was possibly Hispanic. No one besides Ama was black. Or African American, as her teachers preferred to say. She remembered once saying to her second-grade teacher, "I'm from Africa, but I'm just American now." She hadn't yet realized that "African American" was how they felt more comfortable saying "black."

She was getting a sinking feeling about why she had been placed here. Everybody needed a black, er, African American kid. Who cared if she hated the outdoors and yearned for a library? Who cared if this trip was totally unsuited to her and she to it? They probably needed a black kid for the pictures on their Web site.

Jared clapped so loudly that Ama jumped away from him and fumbled her pack. The rest of the group looked over at them.

"This is Ama Botsio. She's from the D.C. area. So our group is complete now—fourteen of you and three of us." He gestured to the two other adults with the GO WILD! T-shirts. One was a woman, late twenties, with frizzy sun-bleached hair and pale bug eyes. The other was an older guy, probably in his late thirties, with a lot of gray in his beard. Ama noticed that their legs were thick and muscled, and their hiking boots looked old and worn. She looked down at her own boots, new, stiff, and blister-giving. Her legs looked almost comically spindly emerging from them.

"That's Maureen, that's Dan. We'll let you all introduce yourselves to each other a little later. We leaders are pretty well outnumbered, as you can see, so you're gonna have to go easy on us," Jared added.

From what Ama could tell, this wasn't a huge problem. Jared looked like he owned the place, and the kids looked decidedly uncomfortable. None of them said a word. Away from their friends and forced to wear ridiculous hiking outfits, even teenagers could be docile.

"Put your packs on the table," Jared said. "We're going

to do an equipment check before we head out. Take your stuff out and put it in neat piles. We'll come around and check the list, all right? Then you can pack up again."

Confused and docile, they lined up at the table and began unpacking. Ama felt her palms sweating. She worked slowly and very neatly as the leaders made their way around the table. She hoped she got Maureen, who was more likely to be sympathetic about hair—though Maureen did not appear to give much thought to her own hair. Ama's hopes sank as Jared appeared. He approvingly ticked off her various ugly woolen things from the list. She held her breath and hoped he would move along the line, but he didn't. He stared at her pack. He seemed to have a sixth sense for equipment fraud.

"Is it empty?" he asked her.

"Uh. Well. I brought an extra book along. Sorry about that. I'll get rid of it." She reached nervously into her pack and brought it out.

He didn't take the bait as hoped. He let her keep her book. "Is that all?"

Ama couldn't lie. She couldn't. She coughed and spluttered.

Jared grabbed her pack and stuck in his arm all the way to the bottom of it. She cringed as he brought out her hair iron and all three packs of batteries. He held the iron up in the air and examined it, which drew many other pairs of eyes to it.

Jared shook his head. "What *is* this thing?"

"It's, uh . . . it's —"

One of the girls tittered, and Ama felt her cheeks burning.

"It's not on the list," Jared said. He picked up a box by his feet that contained a few contraband toiletries, a PSP, two cell phones, and an iPod. He dumped her iron into it, along with the batteries.

She gasped. "You're not going to throw it away?" She thought of Polly, who had bought it for her in sixth grade after seeing it on an infomercial. Ama couldn't let it go. Ama was rational about most things, but not about this.

Jared shook his head. "I'm going to leave this stuff in a locker at the airport. You all can pick it up on your way back. That's why we do this check now and not later."

For a moment, Ama believed she was going to get away with her bottle of Kiehl's Creme with Silk Groom, the finest of fine hair products, her single big indulgence, but Jared was pitiless. He reached into her bag a final time and brought out her precious bottle.

"Please," she begged. "Can I just bring that?"

He shook his head. "The bottle's too big. Once we give you the rest of your equipment, it's not going to fit in your pack."

He glanced at her tragic face. "Listen, if you had a travel size or something, I might let you get away with it, but this is too big."

"I've heard they have a travel size," Ama lamented, half to herself, "but I've never seen it."

He made a move to throw it in the garbage.

"No! You can't throw it away!"

He looked at her as though she'd grown a second set of ears. "Is this really worth storing for almost two months?"

"Yes! Do you know how much it costs?"

He shook his head again. He looked tired. "Fine. You can get it back at the end."

Ama nodded sadly as Jared checked off her name.

"No jewelry!" she heard Jared shout at the next girl in line. Ama smoothed her hair and watched the girl obediently drop her big hoop earrings into the box.

Five

Bryn met Jo at the door of the restaurant, wearing an identical baby blue SURFSIDE T-shirt. "Oh, my God. I'm so psyched! I can't believe you're starting already!"

Jo was psyched too, but also a little nervous. She had no idea what bussing tables involved, though she'd pretended she did on her application. "How's it going so far?" Jo asked under her breath.

Bryn led Jo back to the kitchen. She showed Jo the lockers where the waitstaff kept their purses and stuff and the girls' bathroom, which, according to Bryn, also served as the unofficial girls' lounge.

"That's Megan." Bryn pointed to a girl talking on her cell phone outside the kitchen door. "She's from D.C. She goes to one of the private schools, I think. She's, like, a senior. She's a waitress, so you have to be nice to her and make her job easy so she'll share her tips."

"How do you make her job easy?" Jo asked.

Bryn didn't have time to answer, because she spotted a guy in the dining room. "Do you see that guy?"

"Yeah."

"He goes to South Bethesda."

"Really?" Did anybody work here who wasn't in high school?

"He's a junior. We'll be in school with him next year. Isn't that awesome? Isn't he hot?"

"Uh . . ." He wasn't that hot, Jo didn't think. He was stocky and had very long arms.

"He asked me for a piece of gum yesterday." Bryn looked at Jo expectantly.

"Wow." Jo nodded. "So, what kinds of things are we supposed to do first? Is somebody going to train me?"

"Do you see that girl at the hostess station?"

Jo nodded again. "That's Sheba Crane. She goes to SBH too. She's a sophomore. She's, like, a cheerleader. I'm not kidding."

"Wow." Jo saw how Sheba and the older girls wore their hair up. She made a note to herself to wear hers like that too.

"She could really help us next year. You know?" Bryn

was the same way here as she was in school. She knew who everyone was and what role they were supposed to play.

"You think so?"

"Totally."

"So what time does the shift start?" Jo asked. "I guess those people sitting down over there . . . they're customers, right?"

Bryn didn't look at the customers. She was preoccupied by the two teenage guys who came in the kitchen door at the back, one of whom immediately took off his shirt and tossed it into his locker. By the time that drama was over, there were two more tables of customers and some raised voices in the dining room. Bryn hurried to check it out. She came back looking slightly irritated.

"Jo, come on. You're on section three tonight. You're supposed to do water and bread."

"Hey, Dia?"

Polly's mother was just getting back from her studio the following evening, putting her things down.

"Can I ask you a question?"

"Polly, I'm exhausted and hot. Do you mind if I get a drink first and sit down?"

"Okay," Polly said, following Dia into the kitchen, trying to be patient as she took a bottle of gin from the cabinet and a bottle of tonic from the refrigerator and poured herself a drink. Dia took the glass and sat down at the kitchen table by the window.

Polly slipped into the chair across from her. "How did it go in the studio today?" she asked cheerfully.

Dia shook her head. "It was fine." She took a sip. Polly was hoping to warm her up for conversation, but Dia clearly didn't want to talk about her work today.

The house was completely quiet. Not even the refrigerator was acting up. Sometimes, if it wasn't too late, Dia used to come home from the studio and put on music—raucous punk rock or Bach choral music, usually. But she hadn't in a while and she didn't today.

"What's your question?" Dia asked.

The sun slanted in behind her mother's head, so Polly had to squint to look at her. "Well, when I had chicken soup with Uncle Hoppy he said—"

Dia was shaking her head again. "Right. What did Uncle Hoppy say now?"

"Well, he was telling me about my . . . grandmother."

"What grandmother?"

"You know, my father's mother, I guess it would be."

"Oh, really?"

"Yes, and he said she was really beautiful and . . . did you ever meet her?"

"No. I never met her." Dia had the guarded look she got whenever Polly tried to talk about her father. Polly remembered there was a time when Dia used to like to tell her things about him, like that he was part Romanian. She used to tease Polly that she was very possibly related to Count Dracula. Dia had told her once that her father was good at tennis and bad at dancing, and though he was kind of square, he liked the Sex Pistols. Polly figured that her very existence had probably come about because her father, at least for a time, liked the Sex Pistols.

"But did you know about her? Did you know that she was . . . Uncle Hoppy said—"

"Oh, Polly. I don't know about her." Dia stood up and went back to the refrigerator. "I never met her. I wish that Hoppy wouldn't tell you these things."

Polly didn't want to let it go. "Did you ever see her picture? Did my father ever say anything about her?"

"No. No." Dia turned away.

"He must have! You're not even trying to remember," Polly said.

Polly's mother faced Polly again. "Polly, there is nothing to remember! Do you hear me? I wish Hoppy wouldn't take you out for soup anymore. Next time he calls, you tell him no, okay? He's a sweet old man, but he doesn't know what he's talking about."

Ama had the wrong kind of ankles for hiking. That was what she told herself as she nervously watched the backpack of the next-slowest person disappearing into the trees. She had the wrong kind of everything for hiking. She was tall but thin-boned and delicate. Her body didn't grow muscles like other people's did. Her limbs ached, the skin on her feet blistered easily, her hair defied gravity. What if she got left behind and lost? She tried to pick up her pace, her sholders aching under the straps of her pack, her ankles wobbling over every rock and crevice.

What was this thing, hiking? she wondered. Why did people like it so much? Was it really anything more than just kind of walking along? It seemed to her that there should be more to it than just walking along in order for it to deserve its own name and all this devotion and so much gear.

Her parents had never taken her hiking. They themselves had probably never hiked. She was pretty sure that people in Ghana, real Ghanaians, didn't hike much. She remembered that people in Kumasi, her hometown, walked a lot, and through rough terrain, but the point of it was to actually get somewhere. They called it traveling. Here, it seemed, people had so many cars and buses and subways that walking became practically like a novelty. Hiking was walking for nothing. It was walking for nothing to nowhere and for no reason. With big, uncomfortable boots on.

Was she alone out here? She had to go faster to catch up

to the group. What if she broke her ankle? Would anyone notice or care? Probably only the bears would notice. Maybe wolves. Did they have wolves around here?

She stared at the treacherous ground, which kept tripping her every five minutes. She was the slowest person in the group by a mile. What if she lost the trail? What if she was already going the wrong way? She felt her anxiety mounting. Would she know how to gather food to prevent herself from starving? Would she know which stuff was poisonous? She pictured herself rolling around on the ground after ingesting poisonous mushrooms. She pictured the bears feeding on her carcass.

"In Belgium, I think they call it a butpuck."

Ama startled, jumped, and pivoted. A guy from her group was standing there.

"What?" she said. Her heart was galloping—the only fast thing about her.

He was pointing at her towering pack. "A backpack. The word in Flemish sounds like 'butpuck.' I don't know how you spell it, but that's how you say it."

"Oh." Ama looked down. Where had he come from? What was he talking about? She was terrible at conversing with boys to begin with, and this made for a very difficult opener. She was supposed to laugh, maybe. She felt the seconds tick by. She'd lost her chance to laugh, hadn't she?

"I lived in Belgium until I was in first grade. That's just

an odd fact that stuck in my mind from then." He stopped for a second. "No, wait a minute. Maybe that's not how you say *backpack*. Maybe that's how you say *bathing suit*." He shook his head. "You can see I didn't keep up that well with my Flemish."

His name was Noah, she recalled. He was from New York. He had longish, kind of greasy hair but a very big and very cute smile.

"I lived in Ghana," Ama blurted out, before she could talk herself out of it. "Until I was in first grade."

"Really?"

"Yes."

"My mom worked at a software company in Antwerp," he offered. "That's why we lived there."

"We were just . . . from there," she said. "I mean Ghana. From Ghana." Why was she such a loser?

"Believe it or not, I used to speak Flemish fluently, and now I've forgotten almost all of it. As you can tell. Except *butpuck*, which either means *backpack* or *bathing suit*. Do you still speak . . . what do you speak in Ghana?"

"English, mainly. And a bunch of other regional languages. My family speaks Akan. And my mom's from Côte d'Ivoire, so we speak French, too."

"And you can speak all three?"

She wasn't sure where the line between interesting and abnormal should be drawn. "Yeah," she said uncertainly.

And Spanish and some Arabic, she could have added, but she didn't want to make her family sound like complete freaks. "My parents and my older sister speak them, so I don't really forget. In Ghana most people speak at least two or three languages. It's nothing special."

Ama took a quick look at his face. She was pretty sure she did know where the line between special and boring was drawn, and she wondered why she was in such a hurry to put herself on the wrong side of it.

"Are you here to stay?" he asked. "In the U.S., I mean. Or will you go back?"

"To Ghana? No, I don't think so. My parents have spent their life savings getting us green cards, so I doubt it. Well, I mean, my brother didn't need one. He was born here. He's the American in the family. We all have traditional Ghanaian names and his name is Bob." Ama snuck another look at him. She'd forgotten for a moment that she'd been talking to a boy.

Noah seemed to get a kick out of Bob. He laughed. And suddenly she worried he was laughing at her. Her ankles wobbled.

She realized he had to walk slowly on account of her. He appeared to be as graceful and quiet on his feet as a bobcat, and yet here he was plodding along beside her. He was probably sorry he'd ever stuck himself within a hundred yards of her.

"You can go ahead," she said nervously, tripping. "If you want." She tried to pat down her horrific hair.

"What do you mean?"

"I know I'm slow. You don't have to walk with me."

"I'm sort of going at my own pace," he said. "I took a detour back there and I found a stream and a tiny waterfall. As you can see, I'm not in a big hurry."

"All right," she said warily.

"But if you want to walk by yourself . . . ," he began.

No! I want to walk with you! Please don't go! But she didn't say that. She said, "Whatever."

Six

"No, Mrs. Rollins, I don't mind at all," Polly said as Mrs. Rollins hectically emptied her purse, looking for her car keys. "I don't have to be home until dinner."

Mrs. Rollins almost always needed Polly to babysit at least twice as long as she originally proposed on the phone, and Polly almost always said yes.

"Thanks, Polly." Mrs. Rollins turned to Nicky, her six-year-old, who was playing a game on the kitchen computer. "Nicholas. Did you take my keys?"

Nicky shrugged innocently, though it was a fair question. The kids were frequently attracted to the remote-control aspect of the car keys, especially the red alarm button that made the car go berserk with honking until someone shut it off.

"Katherine!" Mrs. Rollins bellowed up the stairs. "Did you take my car keys?"

Katherine took a minute or two to surface at the top of the stairs. "Huh?"

"Have you seen my keys?"

"No!"

Polly quietly surveyed the kitchen. The main challenge of babysitting for Mrs. Rollins was not Nicky or Katherine but Mrs. Rollins herself. She was always losing her keys or her credit card, always running late, and though she was quite nice and often funny, she talked a lot more and a lot more loudly than anyone in Polly's house.

"Are these them?" Polly asked as she spotted them next to the phone and held them up.

"Yes!" Mrs. Rollins grabbed them out of Polly's fingers and planted a kiss on her cheek. "Oh, my goodness! Polly, what would I do without you?"

Polly smiled. Unlike some grown-ups, Mrs. Rollins had problems Polly found easy to solve.

After Mrs. Rollins left, Katherine materialized from the TV room and Nicky abandoned the computer. They sat on the soft-carpeted floor in the big center hallway, as they often did, and played games. They played cards and Tumblin' Monkeys and the game where the alligator snapped your finger if you pushed on the wrong tooth. Polly always lost that game on purpose and hammed up the pain of the injury, which sent Katherine, who was five, into happy hysterics.

Most teenage babysitters liked to park the kids in front of the TV or the game system and spend the hours talking on their cell phones and texting their friends, but Polly didn't do that. Polly took pride in the fact that Nicky and Katherine almost never watched TV when she was there. They almost never complained or whined. Polly suspected it was because she genuinely liked sitting on the floor, playing with them. She liked their games. She liked drawing pictures at the kitchen table with them. She liked eating chicken nuggets and pudding with them. And not just because she was a good babysitter either. It was what she felt like doing when she was there.

She was serving up the nuggets and mini-carrots when she heard the doorbell. She put down the plates and went to get it.

She opened the door to a tall, very good-looking guy of about twenty. She'd met him at this house before.

"Hey," he said. "Polly, right?"

Polly nodded. She was so amazed and happy that he remembered her name, she was too stunned for a moment to move out of his way and let him in.

At the sound of his voice, the two kids came barreling toward the front door.

"Brian!" they screamed. As he walked in, they both jumped on him at the same time.

He laughed and pretended to lurch and stagger around the front hall.

She watched him pretend-roughhouse with the kids and then effortlessly toss them onto the puffy living room couch one at a time. They were wild with happiness. Brian was their favorite person in the world, she knew.

"Do you want to share our chicken nuggets?" Katherine asked, pulling him by the hand into the kitchen.

"Of course," Brian said.

Nicky leapt onto Brian's back for the walk to the table. Polly passed out more nuggets so there would be enough for everybody.

"I came by to pick up a couple of DVDs for Tibby," he explained, sitting on the table and taking the food Katherine offered. "I told her I'd send them."

Polly nodded. She poured glasses of milk all around.

Tibby was the twenty-year-old sister of Nicky and Katherine, and more than that, she was part of the mythic Sisterhood. She was in college, living in New York City, and Polly had only met her twice. Tibby was a filmmaker, and Polly was so dazzled by her and her reputation that she hadn't managed to say a word in her presence.

Brian was Tibby's boyfriend, though their relationship

was complicated, Polly knew, by his living here and Tibby's living in New York.

For Polly, Brian set the gold standard for boyfriends. When Polly read books or magazine articles involving girls with boyfriends, she found she always pictured Brian.

As much as they worshipped Brian, Nicky and Katherine groused about Tibby sometimes, but that didn't make Polly think any less of her. She understood that kids were perhaps a bit less cute when they were related to you and lived in your house and you couldn't leave them at the end of the day if you wanted to.

When Brian went upstairs, Nicky and Katherine followed, and Polly followed them. She took a hand of each of them and held it, knowing instinctively that Brian wouldn't want them to follow him into Tibby's bedroom.

Brian turned the knob and swung the door open. Polly saw into the room with its shades pulled down, a computer and piles and piles of discs on the desk.

Polly was slightly in awe of this room. The door was mostly kept closed, and though she'd seen into it a few times, she'd never gone in. It was like a shrine to an imagined life, mythical and ominous to Polly. It stood for growing up and leaving home and the artifacts and the people left behind.

On the inside of Tibby's door, Polly noticed, as she had

ónce before, the large photograph of a pale blond girl. It was a close-up picture of the girl's face. The girl was laughing, but there was something haunting to Polly about it, she wasn't sure why.

Polly knew Brian wanted to be alone. "Hey, you two," Polly said to the kids, with the kind of enthusiasm guaranteed to catch their attention. "It's time for me to wreak my revenge in Tumblin' Monkeys. Come on."

Nicky and Katherine easily took her bait and scuttled down the stairs after her.

A few minutes later, Polly had to run back upstairs to get a roll of toilet paper from the linen closet, and she quietly passed Tibby's room again.

Through the half-open door she saw Brian sitting in the dim light on the edge of Tibby's bed. His head was bowed and his elbows rested on his long legs. He held the discs he'd come to find in one hand and his head in the other.

He didn't look up or notice Polly as she hurried along on silent feet, and Polly understood that he sat on Tibby's bed like that because he missed her.

Brian left soon after, and Polly spent the remainder of the afternoon in a trance. Her mind took up its perch near the ceiling and watched her body conduct games of Ants in the Pants and Go Fish.

For some reason she thought mostly about her newly

discovered grandmother who was a model and looked like Sophia Loren, and wondered if that grandmother had ever been loved the way she imagined Brian loved Tibby.

"I don't want to go, but I have to," Jo explained, talking to Bryn on her cell phone while sitting on a bus headed back to Bethesda. "I had to trade shifts with Brownie."

"Brownie's such a loser," Bryn declared. She was never one to forget about the social hierarchy, however much or little it applied.

"Maybe so, but he was willing to give me his shift." Jo's ear was getting hot, so she switched sides. "I'll work lunch tomorrow instead."

"I'm sure he was happy that you even talked to him," Bryn said confidently. She put the phone down for a moment to yell at her brother. "So why are you going back to Bethesda?"

"I'm — I'm having dinner with my dad."

"Really? Why?"

"He . . . he can't come out to the beach because he's . . . you know, on call at the hospital. And he . . . just wanted to see me, I guess."

Jo had worried about how to phrase this. She didn't really understand, herself, why her dad wanted to have dinner, just the two of them, in Bethesda — why he'd almost insisted on it. She didn't want Bryn to push her on this question. Luckily it didn't sound like Bryn was paying close attention. It sounded like she was chewing on something and also possibly typing on her computer.

"Did he just see your report card?" Bryn asked distractedly.

Jo laughed. "Yeah. Maybe that's it." She looked out the window and watched the beach traffic piling up across the highway. She didn't really think that was it.

"I should go," she said. "My phone's gonna die."

"Okay. See ya. Have a blast on the bus."

"You mean luxury motor coach."

"Yeah, that too."

Jo leaned her forehead against the window, watching the deep red sun. Usually it spread its glow all around the sky, but tonight it kept all the color to itself. It looked like it was burning up, falling only a matter of miles to the west of her, on Bethesda maybe, maybe even on her house.

She hadn't called Polly back yet. She should really call Polly. If she told Polly that she was coming home on the bus from Rehoboth to have dinner with her dad, Polly would pay attention and she would instantly see how weird that was.

She remembered, maybe a year ago, when Polly had been talking about her own father, whom she'd never met. "Well, if it makes you feel any better, my father is lost too,"

Jo had said. She'd felt slightly surprised to hear herself say it. She had been in a reckless mood.

"Your dad's not lost," Polly had been quick to say, always literal. "He lives in your house."

"I know," Jo had said, not wanting to say more, but she could see from Polly's face that she did understand, at least partly, what Jo meant.

Jo's dad was a surgeon. When Jo was little, he was still teaching and just beginning his practice. He used to have dinner with the family and take Jo to movies and museums and sports events on the weekends. He practiced violin with her every day. He, more than anyone, taught her how to play soccer. He coached her team until she joined the travel league in fifth grade.

But after Finn, her dad got a lot busier at the hospital. "Your dad's a top surgeon," people were always saying to her, like that should matter a lot. Later they said, "Your dad's a top-top surgeon."

By the time she was twelve, family dinners were a distant memory. With just the three of them, it didn't feel much like a family anymore. Jo ate at Ama's house whenever she could. At home she ate frozen pizzas with Mona, the housekeeper, or takeout with her mom.

Jo and her dad did almost nothing together. Her dad barely even looked at her anymore. He never went into her room. One time when he'd had to fix the toilet in her bathroom, he'd been full of bumbling confusion, like he'd landed on a strange planet. She hoped he did a better job fixing his patients than he'd done fixing the toilet.

"It's hard for fathers to watch their little girls grow up," her grandmother Mary had said.

"I don't think he's watching," Jo had pointed out.

It seemed to Jo that her father was lost in a way that Polly's wasn't. Polly had never had hers, so what was there to lose? "At least he left before he knew you," Jo had said to her. "You can't take it too personally."

Polly had looked stricken on Jo's behalf and obviously hadn't known what to say. She hadn't said anything more on the subject of fathers until a week or so later. "I bet if you needed to have something, you know, removed from you, your dad would be right there."

Jo had tried to laugh, but the laugh hadn't come out. She had instantly changed the subject to zit cream or something. Because Polly had touched on more than she knew. Jo's dad was a top-top surgeon, and he hadn't been able to save Finn.

"Do you know what you want?" Jo's dad asked her over the din of the Mexican restaurant in Bethesda, just two blocks from the station where he'd met her bus.

Jo continued to peruse the many laminated pages of the

72

menu. She was reluctant to give it up, because it was the closest thing to a conversation piece they had.

"I'm still deciding," she said, having taken heed of all specials and also her dad's opinions about what would be good here and what wouldn't be.

She looked around the place. She admired the technique and efficiency of the busboys. These were adults, career restaurant staff, who knew what they were doing—not like the amateurs at the Surfside. She almost wished she could hang around the kitchen and get a few pointers.

"How's the job?" her dad asked her. He put a hand through his hair, which was mostly gray, receding from the temples, with enough reddish blond left to suggest the source of hers. He was wearing a dark suit and looking well-groomed, like the top-top surgeon he was.

She couldn't remember telling him she had a job. Had her mom told him? Had he spoken to her mother about her?

What if she tried to catch him out? *What kind of job do I have?* she felt like asking him. *Okay, then, what's the name of the restaurant?* She pictured him as a contestant on a game show, attempting to answer questions about her life. She imagined the loud buzzer sound when he got the answers wrong.

"It's fine," she said. She'd let him off the hook.

"Good."

He looked pale, she thought. He winced periodically, as though the noise of the place was unlike anything he had ever heard before. She wondered if maybe he wasn't getting out of the hospital much.

They stared at their menus for another minute. The waiter arrived. Her dad looked at her expectantly. He'd grown up in the South, so he would sooner poke her with his fork than order his food before she had.

"I'll have the enchiladas verdes," she pronounced. She ate a chip. She gave up her menu regretfully.

After her father ordered and the waiter went away, they were back in silence. Her father moved his silverware around and she realized she was holding her breath. She couldn't figure out a way to swallow the chip.

"Jo."

"Yes."

"I'd like to talk to you about something."

Here it came. She didn't exactly want to give him permission for the talk, but she couldn't get up and leave either.

"It's about your mother and I."

She chewed her chip. *Me,* she felt like saying. *Your mother and me.* If you were a top-top surgeon you should know that *I* was a subject and not an object. She'd only done her English homework about half the time. She wasn't a top-top anything and even she knew that.

He continued to line things up, including his place mat and water glass. "We are going to start—we're starting a trial separation this summer."

She ate another chip. Maybe two would be easier to swallow than one.

"Your mom is going to stay at the beach with you, and I'm going to be here this summer."

"At this restaurant?" She wished she wasn't saying it, even as she said it.

"At home, Jo."

"Well, that doesn't sound like a big change," Jo said.

He was patient, at least. That was his main good quality these days—not reacting to her, no matter how sassy she was.

"As I said, it is a trial," he continued, wiping his glasses down with his napkin. For a moment she looked at his eyes without the barrier of his glasses. They were deeper, sadder eyes than she expected, and she looked away again. "We'll revisit it in the fall. I'll probably get an apartment near the house if that's what we decide is necessary. Whatever happens, you'll be able to stay in the house."

Was that what mattered to her? Jo wondered. Staying in the house? And anyway, who did the "deciding" about what was "necessary"? What did *necessary* mean? Her dad didn't want to admit that what really mattered was what he wanted, not what he needed. He was trying to make it

75

sound official, but it wasn't official at all. It was what they were choosing.

"We'll still see each other. There won't be any big changes."

If we see each other, that will be a big change, she thought, but did not say.

The food came. Jo carved her enchiladas up very carefully, trying to free the nice, neat pieces from the muck on her plate.

"I get it," she said casually. "That's fine. No big changes. You won't come to the beach. You may or may not get divorced from Mom." She shrugged, but she did not eat.

Jo wondered what her dad had in store, now that he was shaking off the wife and kid. How much had he yearned for this freedom? He was probably going to date the pretty young nurses at the hospital. A top-top surgeon was always in demand. She'd end up being one of those girls whose stepmother was barely older than she was. He'd have parties at the house—no, more likely he'd never be home. He'd sleep on the sofa in his office. He'd go to parties with the residents and wear embarrassing clothes and try to borrow songs off her iPod in an attempt to be cool.

"I hope you'll come home and have dinner with me once a week this summer," he said, in a voice different from the one he'd been using before.

She put her napkin over her mouth and looked down at

her lap. *Not likely,* she thought. *And what would you do if I did? Would you cancel a surgery to see me? Would you really make it home from the hospital in time for dinner?* The one thing this separation would prove was that they were all separated already.

She nodded. "Okay," she said. "No biggie. I'm sure nothing's really going to change."

He nodded too. He looked frankly relieved by her reaction. He'd probably been terrified there would be tears and yelling. He'd probably dreaded that. He was probably thrilled to be off the hook once again. She picked at her food in silence.

As he signaled for the check, she wondered if his patience was such a good thing after all. Maybe she was a jerk to act like she didn't care, but he was a jerk to buy it.

The Latin word
for **willow** is **salix**,
from the verb **salire**,
"to leap."

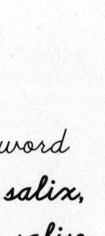

Seven

Ama didn't like to sit too close to the campfire because of the sparks. She had an image of her rowdy heap of hair attracting a spark and setting her whole head aflame in a matter of seconds. She shivered in her fleece. It would be better if she got closer, because she was freezing. But better freezing than aflame, she figured.

She felt embarrassed and stupid that she hadn't helped more with dinner, but she had an irrational fear of can openers. And because of that she hadn't felt entitled to eat much. And because of that she was especially cold and also hungry.

Dan appeared a few yards in front of her, brandishing his camera. He was clearly the trip photographer. "Okay, let's get a campfire picture, group!" he called. "Crowd in a little and smile, would you?"

Ama made a face. There was no way she was crowding in or smiling.

"Say 'cheese'! Say 'marshmallows'! Say 's'mores'!" Dan urged them.

Ama glowered resentfully at the camera, unwilling to look happy or diverse, just as she had done the other times Dan had pointed it at them.

She looked at Noah across the circle. He obliged Dan with a smile and went back to animatedly talking to bug-eyed Maureen. Noah looked really, really nice. Ama was sorry she'd been so puzzling and unfriendly to him for the duration of their walk that afternoon.

Jo always said Ama was mean to boys she didn't like, and Ama guessed that was true. But she suspected she was even meaner to boys she did like.

"I don't like to make a big production about tent mates," Jared was saying to the group as Ama tuned back in to the proceedings. "If the person seated to your right is the same sex as you are, that's your tent mate. If not, look to your left. Otherwise, I'll set you up. No coed tents, please."

Ama was far enough out of the circle that she wasn't quite sitting next to anybody. By the time she crept forward, the girls closest to her were paired up. It reminded her, depressingly, of the many kickball games when she stood waiting until the bitter end to get picked. She tended to do a lot better when the picking was for chemistry experiments or English projects.

"Ama, who's your tent mate?" Jared barked at her over the fire.

Suddenly everyone was looking at her again.

She swallowed. "No one," she said.

"Who still needs a partner?" he asked, looking around the group.

One very tiny boy raised his hand. Ama figured he had to be at least fourteen to have qualified to come on the trip, but he looked more like seven.

"Well, that's not going to work," Jared said. He counted off the group. "We're missing two." He calculated. "We're missing Carly and . . ."

"Jonathan," one of the boys offered.

"Right." Jared looked at Ama. "So you're with Carly. Andrew, you're with Jonathan. Done."

Ama knew who Carly was. She had the large breasts and the loud laugh, and was always getting gum from somewhere.

As Ama wondered where Carly had gone, some singing started up, over by Maureen. *If somebody pulls out a guitar and starts strumming it, I will die,* Ama thought. She decided this was the moment to go pee. She headed off, tentatively, into the darkness. She wanted to get far enough to not be caught or heard peeing, but not far enough to be devoured by wild animals, her screams unanswered.

"*Oh!*" She tripped over something. She staggered a few yards and came down hard.

"Ow! God! Watch it!" a girl's voice hissed at her.

"Sorry," Ama muttered, trying to get her bearings, trying to make her eyes see in the dark. "I didn't realize . . ." Ama's voice trailed off as she tried to stand up.

As her eyes adjusted she saw that she'd plowed into not one person, but two. It was a girl and a boy, and it was pretty obvious what they were doing behind the dense bush. "Sorry," Ama said again.

She crept away in embarrassment. Now she knew where Carly had gone. And Jonathan, too. Ama had the feeling she wasn't getting off to the best start with her new tent mate.

The bus on the way back to the beach was almost empty. Jo's dad wanted her to stay the night at home in Bethesda, but she didn't want to. She'd lied and said her shift started at nine-thirty the next morning and that she couldn't get there in time unless she left that night. He offered to drive her, but she said she was happy to take the bus—anyway, her mom was going to be waiting for her at the bus stop.

It was dark and warm and comforting to feel the miles slipping away underneath her, taking her farther from the Mexican restaurant, closer to somewhere, anywhere else.

It was late enough that most of the beach traffic was gone. It was so dark it almost didn't matter where she was.

Jo curled her feet under her and put her head in her hand. She wanted to prolong the time until her mother would be waiting for her at the bus depot, waiting to see her reaction to the supposedly big news. She wanted to keep living here, in between.

When she leaned her head against the window, she noticed the person sitting in the row across from her and one up. It appeared to be a teenager—a he, not a she. Jo could only see his ear and a part of the side of his face and his shoulder. And even those parts she couldn't see well, because it was pretty dark. But sometimes you could tell, even from seeing a bit of a person, that they were going to be good-looking. This ear was the ear of a very good-looking person, she suspected.

She had leaned over a little more to get a better angle, nearly touching the top of her head to the seat in front of her, when he suddenly turned his face to her. She almost let out a little gasp.

He smiled at her. She sat up quickly, obviously busted. He waved. Feeling stupid, she gave a little wave back. Her heart was pounding.

His ear did not lie. He was very good-looking indeed. She guessed he was a couple of years older than she. *My, what a smile.* Or so it appeared in the dark.

She looked down, wishing to cool her bright pink face, and when she looked up again he was standing in the aisle right next to her.

"Is this seat taken?" he asked gallantly, pointing to the seat next to hers.

She laughed because they were almost the only two people on the bus, amid about fifty empty seats. She laughed because they were halfway to the ocean, and nobody else would be getting on. She probably would have laughed if he had stepped on her foot, because she was feeling punchy and embarrassed. "No," she finally said.

"Do you mind?" he asked, sitting down right next to her.

"No," she said again. She tried to clear her throat. "All yours."

He was very, very cute and he was sitting so close to her she could see his individual eyelashes. One minute she was alone, and now she had him. It was as though she had conjured him right out of her imagination.

"Are you going to the beach?" she asked stupidly, because that was the only place the bus was going.

"No, to Baltimore. Damn, am I on the wrong bus?"

She could see he was teasing her. Only a boy with a smile like his could tease like that. She wished some of the blood throbbing in her cheeks would rise to her brain and give her a bit of intelligence. She had a feeling she was going to need it.

She twisted an earring self-consciously. "I think you'd have more fun at the beach than in Baltimore," she said.

He raised an eyebrow. "Do you? Is that where you are going to be?"

Now she felt stupid again. She figured she could blush and look out the window at pure darkness or she could rise to his challenge.

"In fact, I am," she said.

"Then I must be on the right bus," he said.

She tried not to swallow her tongue. "Me too," she said, a little more timidly than she'd intended.

To her surprise he reached down and picked up her hand. Her eyes widened and her breath stopped as he held it up and compared it in size to his own. "You have nice hands," he said. "Long fingers."

He continued to hold it as though it was a fascinating possession, and she was happy to give it to him. She forgot it was even hers anymore.

When he put it back on her lap, she wished he would take it again. To the rest of her body, her hand was suddenly like a stranger, a prodigal, gone off to have adventures in the big world. But maybe it was like a baby bird that had been held by a human, so it couldn't come home again.

He turned in his seat to face her. His knee touched her knee. He studied her. "You play . . . soccer."

She was surprised yet again. "How did you know?"

He laughed off the mystery. "I can tell you play something. Soccer was the easiest guess."

She nodded, feeling in every way like the easiest guess.

"You swim," she hazarded.

"How did you know?"

She pointed to his head. "The green hair."

She worried for a moment that she'd insulted him, but he erupted into a huge laugh, and she knew she hadn't. She might also have told him she knew he was a swimmer by his broad shoulders, but she didn't think his self-confidence needed any help.

"I use a special product for that. Clairol makes the color. I think it's called fungus. Or seaweed. Or phlegm. Do you like it?"

She laughed. She did like it.

"So, Goldie," he said, tugging on her sleeve. "You come here often?"

"Twice today," she said.

"Really."

"Yes." Barging into her mind were abrupt and disconnected images of her dinner with her dad, the things he'd told her. That was a million miles away from her right now, and it seemed like the right distance.

She didn't want him to ask her more about that, and he didn't. He was looking at her with great intensity, his eyes intimate and conspiratorial. "You're cute as hell," he said.

"*You're* cute as hell," she said back, admiring her own nerve.

She felt the warmth of him as he came closer.

Was he going to try to kiss her, just like that? Was she going to let him?

She didn't feel like herself. She felt like she was playing herself in a movie. Except in the movie, she was the kind of person who would flirt with a very gorgeous stranger on a bus and even kiss him. It was a pretty good movie, she thought, as she felt his cheek against hers, briefly, and then his lips on hers.

The first kiss was soft, like a question, and when he saw that she was neither shocked nor unwilling, he put a hand on either side of her face and kissed her more deeply. The back of her head pressed against the seat. Boldly she put her palm against his warm neck. She felt his hair tickle the back of her hand and felt his pulse in her fingertips. Or maybe it was her pulse. His breath was like steam. Or maybe that was her breath. With her other hand she felt the softness of his shirt, sort of a knit sweatshirt-type thing with a string at the neck and a wooden toggle, the kind that skaters, swimmers, and stoners wore.

He kissed her chin and under her chin and along her neck. She thought she would surely die or explode. Explode and then die. *I can't believe what is happening in this movie,* she thought distantly.

She was just a bunch of nerve cells, living on the very surface of herself. His lips were warm and confident and made hers that way too. She'd often worried about being an incompetent kisser if it ever came to it, but her mouth seemed to know what to do. His mouth had enough confidence for both of theirs.

She was faintly aware of the bus swerving off Highway 1, making the exit to Rehoboth. When the bus stopped, they broke apart. He gave her a sly look and one last hard kiss.

"This is Rehoboth Beach," the driver bellowed.

The front door of the bus swung open. He helped her get her bag and watched her go stumbling up the aisle. She hoped he wasn't getting off here but was staying on to Dewey Beach or Bethany or Ocean City. It would be too awkward to face him outside the bus, to act like strangers or, alternatively, introduce him to her mom. She didn't even turn around to find out. She kept her gaze rigidly ahead; her limbs were shaky and her heart thumping wildly.

She felt like she was drunk and also underwater. She tried to shake her head to sober up. She saw her mother waiting in the car and tried to push herself back up through miles of heavy water to the air.

What did you do? she asked herself, sucking in the moist, cool beach breeze. *How did that just happen?*

She wished so much she could walk home, holding on to her heady buzz, rather than get into the car with her mom and lose all of it. Would her mom see her flushed face and her shaking hands and know immediately that something was up? She felt like she was wearing her brain inside out.

What were you thinking? she asked herself, but apparently herself didn't feel much need to answer.

Dear Grace,

I'm trying to think of something good to say about all this. I really am. It's a lot easier to think of the bad stuff. Like my blisters, my horrifying hair (my Kiehl's and my battery-powered iron were confiscated the first day), my slutty tent mate, the agony of campfire singing, the food, the dilapidated bus, many horrible miles of hiking, and my flatulent cooking partner (flatulent means he farts a lot—may or may not appear on SAT). That's just the beginning. Also, no one likes me, and I don't like anyone.

Oh, wait, I thought of something. I like gorp. Gorp is a food. (People who hike and camp like to give a special name to everything.) It's a combination of nuts, raisins, and M&M's. Well, I like the M&M's, anyway. I guess I already knew that about myself.

I don't mean to complain, but I can't help it. The days go so slowly and there are so many to go.

How's Andover? I wish I were there.

xoxoxo
Ama

P.S. My tent mate, Carly, has made out with three different boys in four days. I am not exaggerating.

Dear Maman,

All is well here. I am learning a lot and the days are very full. Please give Papa and Bob my best love. Tell Esi hi from me when you talk to her.

Love,
Ama

Eight

"Hey, Dia?"

Polly made a point of catching her mother in the short window of time between when she woke up and when she left the house for her studio.

Dia looked up from her large mug of coffee. Her eyes were still slightly crossed and baggy from sleep.

"Are you pouncing? No pouncing."

That was a cardinal rule of the morning. Polly got up early and Dia slept late. By the time Dia got up, Polly was bursting with pent-up conversation. It was hard for her to stay quiet as Dia stumbled through her morning routine.

"No. I was . . . I was just going to ask you something,"

Polly said defensively. She rubbed her sock feet together under the kitchen table.

"Okay. Fine."

"Could I go to modeling camp in Gaithersburg in late July?"

"*What?*"

"Modeling camp. It's only half an hour away. I looked on the map. I can pay for most of it from babysitting. It's just a day camp, nine to four Monday through Friday. And it's only for two weeks. Several real supermodels went there."

"*Modeling camp?*"

"Yes." Polly broke her toast into pieces with her fingers.

"What is modeling camp?"

"It's where you . . . you know, learn to be a model."

"Or just look like one," Dia muttered.

"What?" Polly asked.

"Nothing. Where did you get this idea? Are your friends going to model camp?"

"No." Polly had told her mother several times what Jo and Ama were doing for the summer, but she must have forgotten. "I found it on the Internet."

"Why?"

"Why did I find it?"

"I mean, why were you looking? Do you seriously want to be a model?"

Polly broke her toast into smaller pieces. Going into this conversation, Polly had had a feeling that her mother wasn't going to be one hundred percent supportive. Dia was always saying how she was a feminist and how Polly was too. Dia didn't like celebrity magazines or most TV shows because she said they were degrading to women. Polly did like those things, and she was secretly worried she wasn't a feminist.

"Well, I think it could be interesting," Polly said quietly.

Dia's face softened a little. She took a long sip of coffee. "Do you think you have the right look for it? Aren't models supposed to be really tall?" she asked.

"I'm still growing," Polly said. "I could be tall."

"Polly, I'm five two. You're taller than me, but you've never been tall."

Polly wanted to ask about her father, *Was he tall?* But she was afraid it would only hinder her chances.

"Some models aren't tall. Like . . . hand models."

"You want to be a hand model?"

"No. Well, I don't know." Polly was an inveterate nail biter. She made her hands into fists.

Dia sighed. She looked tired. "You don't have enough to do this summer, do you?"

"No, it's not that. I just thought that this could be . . . interesting."

"Polly, modeling is not interesting. You are interesting. You are too interesting for modeling, in my opinion. Do you really want to be judged just on how you look?"

"I think there's a lot more to it than that," Polly said. "It's like . . . acting, actually." She went back to work on her toast. "And you learn about fashion. Which I'm pretty interested in. And it said on the Web site you can learn about photography and fitness."

"Polly, you are getting crumbs everywhere."

Polly abandoned her toast and tried to dust her hands off carefully over her plate. "Please, can I please go? I can take the Metro there and back on my own. You don't need to do anything."

Dia sighed again, more loudly this time. "I don't know," she said, but she got the look of resignation Polly was aiming for. It used to take longer to get Dia to the resignation stage, but Polly had refined her technique.

"I'll think about it," Dia said.

"Okay," Polly said. She was smart enough not to allow herself any expression of triumph. *I'll think about it* meant yes. *Maybe* meant probably. *No* meant it would take some more work on Polly's part to convince her.

"Why aren't you eating breakfast?"

Polly stuck one of the mangled bits of toast into her mouth. "I am."

• • •

Jo woke up that morning with a kissing hangover. Her lips felt swollen, her cheeks felt raw, and her conscience stung a little. She had heard about this kind of hangover before, but she had never had one.

"Joseph, you're on flatware this shift," commanded Jordan, the pimply, solitaire-playing assistant manager who wouldn't have hired her. He liked to send her into the kitchen to load and unload the silverware whenever one of the dishwashers failed to show up.

Jo nodded distractedly at him and veered toward the kitchen, train of thought unbroken.

"*Hola*, Hidalgo," she said to the fry cook, who was standing at his locker.

It wasn't like she had never kissed anyone before. She'd kissed Arlo Williams several times at parties. He had been more nervous than she was.

Arlo's kissing was different, though. It didn't cause the swelling or the stinging. Kissing Arlo was maybe like drinking one beer, whereas kissing . . .

Wait a minute. Jo winced. Kissing . . . whom? What was his name?

Oh, my God, did she really not know his name? Had he told her and she'd forgotten? No, she would have remembered it. Had she told him hers? Had she really landed a severe kissing hangover and never even bothered to introduce herself?

Wow. She couldn't help thinking of Ama. What would Ama say? She didn't want to think about that. She pictured Bryn, whom she'd see later at the dinner shift. Bryn would understand. *He was gorgeous,* Jo would say, and that would be explanation enough. In fact, she was a little bit excited to tell Bryn about it, because Bryn would be excited about it too. Maybe Jo wouldn't mention the fact that she didn't know his name. That was kind of a hoochie move, even for a person like Bryn.

Jo began unloading the clean silverware from the night before. She mindlessly sorted the pieces in the cart, glad it was still early and no one else was in the kitchen. She was happy to have some time to herself. She was grateful that her mom had still been asleep this morning when she'd left the house for a run on the beach and then a swim in the ocean. She'd snuck into the outdoor shower to clean up and dress for work and left without being seen.

"Did he tell you?" Those were the only words her mother had said to her on the ride home from the bus the night before. Jo had nodded and that had been it. Jo had gone to bed not thinking about her mother or her father or what he'd told her. She'd fallen asleep thinking of kissing on the bus.

She shut the door to the giant commercial dishwasher with a bang and a shudder.

So she had kissed a stranger. So she didn't know his name. Everybody was allowed a random, possibly misguided kiss once or twice, weren't they? There weren't any real consequences to a kiss.

No, there weren't. And besides that, it was over and done. She was never going to see the guy again in her life, and maybe that was for the best.

"Ama, you ought to loosen up a little." That was what Jared had said to her after breakfast. Now, hours later, Ama was still thinking about it. Jared wasn't the first person to say that to her in her life. Jo had said it. Polly hadn't said it outright, but Ama suspected she had thought it. Grace didn't say it. The other kids in her accelerated math class never said it. Her parents didn't say it and her sister certainly didn't.

What did it mean, anyway? What was so good about being loose? Could you get perfect grades if you were loose? Could you master four languages? Could you get into Princeton or get a full scholarship through medical school?

Maybe looseness was one of the many things Ama couldn't afford, like movie candy and Seven jeans. Maybe being loose was like hiking—only an idea, and from a practical standpoint, completely useless.

Over the dying embers of the postdinner campfire, Ama sensed Noah looking at her. Her face burned, but she couldn't look back. She pictured her hair. *I would smile at him if my hair wasn't this bad. I would talk to him. Definitely.*

97

"We're going to be working up toward the final rappel," Dan, the bearded guy, was telling the yawning group. They had hiked eight miles through dense forest, and Ama had a pain and a blister for every one of them. "It's three hundred fifty feet, give or take, so we want to get you guys comfortable with the ropes and the gear, and also with that kind of height."

Ama raised her hand. Dan looked over at her. "Ama, you don't need to raise your hand here."

Ama pulled it down, embarrassed. It wasn't the first time she'd been told that, either. She cleared her throat. "What's a rappel?"

"It's the safest, fastest way to get down a cliff or a steep mountain face. We secure your rope to the top of the rock, and your belayer feeds you the rope as you go down. We ask that you take it slowly," he said, looking meaningfully at Jonathan, who was reckless.

Ama held her own hand so she wouldn't raise it again. "What's a belayer?" she asked.

"Your belayer is your trusted partner. He or she makes sure your rope is secure and lets it out slowly as you descend. Be nice to your belayer, whoever he or she may be. He holds your life in his hands."

Ama felt a stab of terror. Had she been nice to anyone? Whom here could she trust with her life? She pictured herself catapulting down the mountain to a painful death.

"The rappel is kind of like your final exam," Maureen explained. "It's a big part of your grade. We want to start with some climbing tomorrow to make sure you're all ready for it."

Ama felt her ears ringing. Her hand was halfway up before she could retrieve it. "What do you mean grade?"

"Your grade for the course," Maureen said.

"Your grade for the course? You get a grade for the course?" Ama's voice was anything but loose.

"If you're taking it for high school credit, as most of you are. We're required to give you a grade. It's not my preference, but that's how it is."

"So you get a grade from this and it goes on your transcript?" Ama persisted.

"If you are getting credit, yes."

"Can you take the course for credit but not get a grade, you know, just get a pass, like you get in gym?"

"No, Ama, you can't. You get a grade."

"And you have to throw yourself off a mountain to get a good one?"

"We call it rappelling," Maureen said patiently.

Later that night Ama lay in her sleeping bag and worried. The night air was humid and made the fabric of her sleeping bag feel slightly damp against her skin. Absently she watched the shadows passing over the orange nylon walls of the tent, wondering if they represented man or beast or teenager.

What if her first grade in high school was an F? How could she live that down? She couldn't. She couldn't even imagine what her parents would say.

In normal circumstances, Ama loved grades. She loved the concreteness of them. She was the kind of person who felt disappointed when a teacher said "Don't worry, you won't be graded on this."

She mostly loved grades because all the grades she got were As. She loved As. She loved the way they looked, the straight and pointy aspect of them in contrast with the weak curves of Bs and Cs. But how could she possibly get an A in this? She couldn't. It was wrong for her. She was wrong for it. What if her first high school grade was a B or, God forbid, a C? Or worse! It could easily be worse! Ama could barely breathe at the thought of it. What would Esi say?

She thought of the rappel. And how it was only going to get worse.

Around midnight, she guessed, Carly snuck into the tent with a boy. Ama froze in her sleeping bag. She didn't dare lift her head.

"Don't worry, she's asleep," Ama heard Carly whisper.

"Are you sure?" the boy asked.

Ama thought it sounded like Jonathan. Carly was back to Jonathan.

"Yeah, she always falls asleep early."

No, I am not asleep! Ama felt like shouting. *How can I sleep when my first high school grade is going to be an F?* She squeezed her eyes shut as she realized, to her disbelief, that the two of them were climbing into Carly's sleeping bag together, giggling. She wished she had sat up and said something right away, but now what was she supposed to do? She lay there motionless, barely breathing.

"Did you hear her going nuts over her grade tonight?" the boy, probably Jonathan, said. "Dude, that girl is so freaking uptight. How do you share a tent with her?" He said something else, but softer and mumbled, so Ama couldn't hear it. She felt the pulse of outrage and tingle of humiliation climb all the way up her scalp.

Ama badly wished she was asleep. Or really anywhere else in the universe. She hated this place.

She heard the zip of Carly's sleeping bag and Carly giggled again. Ama heard more giggling and whispering.

"She's not that bad," Ama overheard Carly say.

Nine

J o stretched out the time it took to get home from the restaurant that night. When she walked through the front door she felt like she was walking into a different kind of house. She heard her mother vacuuming in the living room and knew that her dad wouldn't be coming home that night or Friday night or any night. She tried to keep those thoughts away, but there they were.

Just because her father was coming for no nights this summer instead of ten or twelve, it made this a different kind of place. It turned this house into her mother's place and turned Jo into an article of custody.

There was so little—ten or twelve nights—that made this anything like a family house. The slightest nudge and it came apart. So then, what was the big deal? What was the big difference? What did it really matter? An idea had changed, maybe. A classification had changed. But nothing that was real had been lost.

"I'm only sorry you're there in the middle of it," her aunt Robin had said when she'd caught Jo on her cell phone during her break at the restaurant that afternoon.

"You don't need to be sorry," she'd told her aunt. "I am fine." There was no being "in the middle of it." There was no middle. Her dad was in one place, her mom was in a different place. There was nothing new in that.

She went to her room and picked up her dirty socks and emptied her garbage can. She carefully folded her Surfside T-shirt and left it on the top of her dresser for tomorrow. She stared forlornly at the single handprint she'd made on the window. She was going back to being a tourist here.

Dear Esi,

They give a grade for this course! I am freaking out! It's going to be my first high school grade. I asked one of the leaders if you could take it pass-fail. She didn't even answer me. Why can't I be at Andover, where I belong? Why am I here? What did I do wrong in my life to deserve this?

And besides that, my tent mate Carly made out with a guy in our tent! With me in it! They thought I was asleep, but I wasn't! Can you believe that? What a slut! I had to listen to them and it was disgusting! At least they didn't start taking their clothes off or anything. Dan, one of the leaders, must have heard something, because he shouted for everyone to get in their tents and shut up.

How come nothing like this ever happens to you, Es?

Love,
Ama

After Ama completed this letter she crumpled it up and tossed it into the cooking fire. Even Ama had her limits. Anyway, what was the point? They wouldn't hit another mail drop for five days.

As they began the day's endless, pointless hike, Ama stared suspiciously and unwaveringly at the ground. She had to keep a very close eye on it, because it was always coming up with a new way to make her stumble. For her grade, she was supposed to be looking at tree types, but she didn't dare. She'd have to learn to recognize them by their roots.

She was seeing a lot of bugs. And also slugs. There were a lot more slugs in the world than she had ever guessed. She paid special attention to the bugs and ants, because she was trying to figure out which kinds could bite or kill her. If she was given her grade on bugs, she might do well.

Jared had given her something called moleskin for her blisters and an extra pair of socks he'd brought along. "Man, Ama. These are some of the worst blisters I've seen. I don't know how you are walking."

The moleskin had helped for the first five miles, but she could feel from the wetness in her boots that the blisters had started to bleed again.

By the sixth mile she had fallen far behind, and during the seventh she was stunned to actually catch up. As she came upon the group, they were clustered together in a clearing, bathed in late-day light, all of them looking up at something.

"What's going on?" she asked Maureen, lifting off her heavy pack and easing it to the ground.

"We're taking a break before the last part of the hike. We're camping up there tonight."

"Up there?"

"Up there."

"On that *mountain*?"

"Yes. It's only a mile from here, but it's all up."

Ama felt tears fill her eyes and tried not to blink them

out. How could she get up that mountain? She pressed her lips together so they wouldn't tremble. She looked at her pack. She looked down at her feet. How could she do it?

She realized the other kids were putting their packs back on. No! Not already! It was one of the many bad things about being the slowest hiker: the break was always ending by the time you caught up. If she took the time to drink or eat, she'd be lost. She'd never catch up again.

"Are you okay?"

Noah was looking at her.

She tried to ease the stricken look from her face. "I'm okay."

"Do you need some help?"

"No, I'm okay," she choked out. She was about to cry. All of a sudden she realized this, and that she was going to be unable to stop it.

"Excuse me," she muttered. She stumbled toward a clump of trees. She kept going until she was out of eyesight and earshot.

She cried only until she could make herself stop. Then she blew her nose on a leaf and straightened up. When she got back to the clearing the group had left. They were already snaking in a line up the mountain. She looked around frantically for her pack, but it wasn't there. Where was it? Hadn't she left it there?

Oh, my God! What would she do without her pack? Her

106

sleeping bag? Her clothes? Her water? Should she tell the leaders? How many more ways could she find to mess this up?

She squinted at the hikers on the trail. She realized as she studied them that a tall one toward the front of the line, namely Noah, was carrying not one pack but two.

"Did you see the new waiters?" Bryn asked Jo the next afternoon when Jo emerged from the kitchen, shiny, pink, and damp with steam from the dishwasher's drying cycle.

"No. Why?"

"You'll see when you see them," Bryn said suggestively.

Each weekend, as the summer progressed and the restaurant got busier, the management took more waitstaff.

"It'll get as big as it gets by the Fourth of July," Caroline, a veteran of many summers, had explained to Jo. "In August servers will start having fights and leaving and getting fired."

Jo was doubtful about what she'd see, and amused by the pure boy-craziness of Bryn, but she took off the kitchen apron anyway.

"Did you see the new waiter?" waitress Megan asked her as she sat down at the staff table to eat a crab roll before the dinner shift started.

"No. Why do people keep asking that?"

Megan raised her eyebrows. "Because he's cute. Both are cute, but one is *really* cute."

Jo took a bite of her roll and chewed. "I'm retired from cute boys," she said through a half-full mouth.

Megan looked amused. "Really?"

"Yeah."

"You're pretty young for that, aren't you?"

Jo tried to look serious. "I've had my share."

Megan laughed. She was big and strong-looking, like she played field hockey or something, but she had a gentle face.

Jo looked up at the clock and realized she had less than a minute until table-setting time. She shoved the remaining half of her crab roll into her mouth and got up from the table. She nearly collided with two large people entering the room, no doubt the famous new waiters. When she looked up at the two faces she discovered, to her astonishment, that only one of them was a stranger. The other one was indisputably familiar, especially around the mouth.

Jo's cheeks were full of food and her eyes big in their sockets. She backed up a few feet. She stared, trying to chew and swallow.

The familiar one, whose name she did not know, took a moment to process the unexpected familiarity of her as well. She was hard to place, probably, what with it being so light out and her being more than three inches from his face.

She watched as his confused surprise gave way to happy surprise.

"Goldie?" he said.

She swallowed the last of her crab roll and tried to clear her airway. "It's Jo," she coughed out.

"You work here?" he asked.

Megan and Bryn materialized at her side. "You two know each other?"

"Sure," he said with a big smile.

"Sort of," Jo said, looking at her foot.

Polly didn't have a decent mirror in her room, so she listened at her door for total silence before creeping into the hallway in her bra and underwear. She darted into the bathroom and closed the door behind her. The big mirror was high above the sink in the bathroom, so she had to hoist herself up to get a good look at herself in it.

She looked at herself and herself looked back.

Strange, in a way, that that person she saw was this person she was. She didn't necessarily feel like that person. Mostly she went about her life with no concept of what she looked like. Looking at herself now, she didn't quite square up.

Did that mean she was not good model material?

She pretended the mirror was a camera. She smiled at it. Hmmm.

She could get those teeth-whitening strips. That could help. Not so much with the overbite, but with the whiteness.

She got up on her knees, balancing on the edge of the sink so she could see more of her body.

Though she had never said it out loud to anyone, her bra size was 34D. Somehow she thought that by not saying it and by standing in a certain way, she could make the world believe that she wore a 34B like everybody else.

She hoped she was still growing vertically, but she sincerely hoped she was done growing there. If she lost weight, she would probably get smaller. And also there was a surgery you could get to make them smaller if worst came to worst.

She wondered if her grandmother had worn a size 34D. Back then, having big ones was probably more acceptable in models.

Polly's lips were big. Her eyes were dark and big. Her nose was not-small. Her waist was small, but her hips stuck out. Sometimes Polly felt jealous of the girls with tiny features and straight-up-and-down bodies and nothing sticking out anywhere. Polly felt like everything of hers stuck out everywhere.

Her skin was pale and almost completely clear. That was one thing she had going for her. She leaned in closer and saw two tiny pimples on her chin. Oh, well. There was makeup for that. Everyone knew models wore tons of makeup.

Her knees were hurting against the porcelain and she still didn't have the whole picture, so she stood up, slowly, teetering to her full height with one foot on either side of the basin. She looked up and saw that the top of her head was only a few inches from the ceiling.

Oh, no. Her underwear was atrocious. Why was she still wearing those? They were old cotton briefs with faded purple flowers. Models did not wear Carter's briefs. There was no way she could evaluate the state of herself wearing that underwear.

She scrambled down off the sink so she could throw them away and find another pair. She strode back to her bedroom, pulled open the top drawer of her bureau. She took out a respectable pair of red bikini underwear she'd gotten with Jo at Victoria's Secret last year. She pulled off the old ones and put on the new.

But with her hand poised to throw the old ones in the wastebasket, she began to slow down and rethink. Now that she was back in her old, dim room and not immediately faced with her glaring face, she started to feel sorry for her old purple-flowered briefs. They were very soft.

111

They had been washed hundreds of times, and still they had no holes and none of the elastic had sprung out of them. They had been very nice to her the whole time she'd had them. In truth, they were probably her most comfortable pair. Not all underwear was comfortable. Jo had gotten her to wear a thong once with her leggings, and that was *not* comfortable, no matter what anybody said.

Polly couldn't just throw them away for no good reason. What had they ever done wrong? They couldn't help it if they weren't sleek or fashionable. They just were how they were.

Instead of throwing them away, she folded them up into a tiny ball and put them away in the back of her drawer.

Okay, so she wouldn't throw them away just yet. But she would *not* wear them. Unless there were absolutely no other clean ones. And she would *not* wear them to modeling camp.

It took Ama hours to thank Noah. She kept trying to think of a way. She hovered close enough to him on several occasions to say the two words, but she couldn't make herself do it.

Later, she went by herself to a stream to peel off her pus-soaked, bloody socks in privacy. It turned out Noah was there too, washing some clothes.

"Thank you," she blurted out, before the words could crawl back down her throat and hide.

"No problem," he said.

She tried to submerge her feet and rinse her socks before he could see, to spare him the gruesomeness, but she didn't quite get them under in time.

He openly winced at the sight of them, and she didn't blame him. Between her hair and her feet she was a genuine fright. She'd give him nightmares for sure.

Earlier that evening, as she'd walked the last mile feeling as light as a bird without her pack, she'd had an idea. It was so comforting it had carried her up to the top of the mountain. Maybe Noah could be her belayer. If he was her belayer, she had the hope that maybe she wouldn't absolutely die.

It was a good plan with one major problem: she would have to find a way to ask him to be her partner, and she knew she never would.

The bark of the
willow contains
salicylic acid,
the source of
aspirin, and has
relieved fever and
suffering for
thousands of years.
It also gets rid
of warts.

Ten

"I heard he has a girlfriend," Sheba said, her loud voice amplified by the slick tiled walls and metal stalls of the women's bathroom/lounge at the Surfside.

Jo stopped her hand-washing mid-lather.

"Who told you that?" a waitress named Violet Brody asked.

"Uh, I forget. . . . Did you tell me that, Megan?" Sheba asked.

Megan put down her eyeliner and turned from the mirror. "I didn't say that. I don't think he has a girlfriend. If he did, would he be looking at Goldie"—she pretended to cough—"excuse me, looking at *Jo*, like he wanted to eat her in one bite?"

Jo stared straight ahead, frozen. It was the end of the night, and the older girls had gathered in customary fashion to brush their hair and put on makeup for their late-night activities. Usually Jo and Bryn hung out in the girls' room as long as they could, soaking up the atmosphere and the gossip. Once the older girls left, they washed up and walked the boardwalk for a little while and then went home.

"He does seem to have a thing for Jo, doesn't he?" Violet said, as though Jo wasn't even there.

"You know him from somewhere, right?" Megan asked, turning to the actual Jo instead of just talking about her.

"Well," Jo began, startled to be the center of attention. *Not so much that I know his name.* "We met one other time." *Specifically the night before last.* She turned off the water and dried her hands.

"I can't believe you know him!" Bryn squealed.

"I guess you made a big impression," Sheba said.

"He's a little old for her, isn't he?" Violet asked.

Jo had no idea how old he was. Her face burned with embarrassment and also some amount of pride. All eyes were on her.

"Not more than a couple years. Maybe three," Megan said.

"It's not that he's too old for Jo," Sheba said to Megan,

resuming the version of the conversation where Jo wasn't there. "He's too . . . cool for Jo."

Bryn laughed a little too loudly.

"Thanks a lot," Jo piped up.

"Not too cool. I mean, too slick," Sheba amended. "He seems like a player, doesn't he?"

"Possibly," Megan said.

"Likely," Violet added.

"He looks like trouble," another waitress, named Caroline, agreed.

"But he's so hot!" Bryn opined, eager to stay in the conversation.

Jo watched them gather up their things and drift out of the restaurant. Jo and Bryn were left to themselves. She could still hear the older girls discussing the potential of her and him. It didn't seem to make any difference that she was no longer among them.

The terrain got rockier over the next two days. The group did their first technical climb, which meant they used ropes.

Ama's entire body shook for the hour leading up to her turn. She haltingly climbed five feet off the ground, looked over her shoulder, and panicked. Her hands clung so hard to the rope she burned the skin of her palms. Her feet shook so hard she couldn't make the toes of her boots stick in any of the holds.

Eventually Dan and Jared had to pull her up by the rope, nothing more than dead weight. When she got up to the top she thanked them, walked a few feet away, and vomited.

Later, after eating lunch and resting in the sun for a while, she looked out over the rock face they'd climbed. She stood a good distance back from the edge, of course, and tried to calculate its height. She figured it was probably similar in altitude to the final rappel. Maybe a little lower, but not much.

Later still she sat on a flat rock as Maureen rubbed salve into her cut-up hands.

"How far was that climb?" Ama asked casually.

Maureen held up both of Ama's wrists to examine her hands in the fading sun. "Yikes, girl," she murmured. "How did you do this much damage?"

Ama shrugged. *You should see my feet,* she thought. "So do you know? How far it was?"

"The climb today?" Maureen asked. "Maybe forty feet."

"Forty feet?" Ama exploded. "That's all?" She balled up her sore hands.

"Could be forty-five. Not as much as fifty." Maureen looked perplexed.

"Not as much as fifty? Feet? You mean feet? Not meters?"

"I mean feet." Maureen studied her. "Ama, what's wrong?"

Ama clamped her jaw shut. "Nothing," she whispered.

The final rappel was *350 feet*! That was seven times higher than the climb today. *At least* seven times higher. Maybe more like nine.

Ama walked a few feet away and vomited again.

"You're going *where*?" Jo asked, sitting up in her lounge chair.

"To modeling camp," Polly answered. "I wrote you that in one of my e-mails, didn't I?"

"I don't think I got that," Jo said guiltily. "What is modeling camp?"

"It's in Gaithersburg."

"Not where is it. *What* is it?" Jo practically shouted into her cell phone. "What do you do there?" The truth was, Jo had finally returned Polly's call at a time when she believed Polly would be busy babysitting or something, but instead Polly had eagerly picked up on the first ring. Jo was already frustrated with Polly before she'd even said hello.

"You learn about modeling. All kinds of things, I guess."

"Like what?" Jo saw her mother appear on the spacious deck at the back of their house in her big straw hat and her black bikini. Jo looked away. It was a lot more of her mother than she felt like seeing.

"I don't know. Fashion, makeup. You know, photography and stuff." Polly's voice got quieter. She sounded less confident the more she spoke.

Jo made herself stop and breathe. "I didn't mean to sound negative. I just didn't realize they had a camp for that."

"Is it because you don't think I could be a model?"

Jo heard that plaintive sound in Polly's voice and forced herself to quiet her impulses. If it had been Ama, she could have been honest. *No way! You don't look anything like a model.* Ama was tough in that particular way. Then again, if she'd been talking to Ama, the honest answer would have been *Sure, go for it,* because Ama actually did look like a model. But she couldn't tell Polly what she really thought. Polly was not tough in that way.

"Polly, I don't know. I'm no expert."

"Do you think I have the wrong look?" Polly sounded so sad and serious, Jo almost caved in.

But Polly did have the wrong look. She had big boobs and a wasp waist. She had big features, serious cheekbones, and an overbite—the kind of face you had to grow into. Polly was beautiful in a weird way, but not in a way that most people recognized.

"Polly, I think that you are going to be a slow cooker, you know? In, like, twenty years, you're going to be a lot prettier than those modely-looking girls, I bet."

Polly was quiet for a moment, and Jo found herself hoping that this would do the trick.

"But Jo, you can't start being a model when you're in your thirties."

Jo bit her own knuckle. "Polly. I'm not just talking about being a model."

"Well, I'm just talking about being a model," Polly said.

"Okay, okay. Listen, have fun at the camp. I didn't mean to sound negative."

"So you think it could work out? The modeling idea?"

"Sure," Jo said wearily. "Why not." It was a small capitulation. What did it matter? It would get Jo off the phone, if nothing else.

Jo was exhausted. She was confused. She was depressed by the sight of her bikini-clad mother trying to scrub two spots of white paint off the deck railing, her new tummy tucked for all to see. Jo was depressed that Polly could be so optimistic about things that weren't going to go her way.

Including Jo. Polly remained optimistic about staying really close, and sometimes Jo just wanted her to ease up.

Sometimes being friends with Polly felt like being friends with her younger self, like she knew what was going to happen and that it wasn't going to be good. Jo wanted to keep going forward, and Polly always pulled her back.

• • •

"Goldie!"

Jo walked out the back of the Surfside after a late dinner shift and two tables in her section who kept ordering pitchers of beer and would not leave. She thought everybody except Jordan and Hidalgo were already gone, but a certain person materialized at her side just beyond the Dumpsters.

"Hi," she said shyly.

He wasn't shy at all. He grabbed her hand and kissed her knuckle. He put both hands on her waist and kissed her jaw. "I've been wanting to do that all night. Do you want to go get something to eat?"

She thought of the warning of the older girls in the bathroom. Did anybody see that? Was she going to hear about it tomorrow? She thought of her curfew and her mother waiting for her.

He kept her hand and pulled her along the boardwalk.

"I have to be home soon," she protested. She didn't want him to think she was the kind of girl who would just start kissing him in any old place at any time. Even though he had pretty good reason to think that.

"It won't take long." He stopped at the first fudge stand and ordered the assorted half-pound. He paid for it with newly earned tip money. "See? I got dinner," he said, holding up the box proudly. "Let's go eat it on the beach and then I'll take you right home."

She followed him down onto the sand, a sense of fun building in her heart. It was a Sunday night beach, dark and deserted, just the way she could least resist him. He pulled her close as they sat down on the sand, just beyond the surf. The air was sweet on her skin, warm but not hot. He opened the box of fudge and handed her a piece. "This kind is good. It's got peanut butter, I think."

"Very nutritious dinner," she said. She was shaking a little. She heard the giddiness creeping into her voice.

"Nutrition is important to me," he said.

She took tiny bites of hers. She was too excited to eat.

He took a green one from the box and examined it suspiciously. "What is this, do you think? Fudge should not be green." He drew his arm back and tossed it far into the ocean.

"Hair should not be green," she said softly, knowing it was dangerously flirtatious.

He laughed delightedly and turned to her in a way that she knew meant he was going to kiss her. He kissed her. What could she do?

Couldn't you be more . . . awkward? she wondered of him. How did he just get her kissing him like this without even having to suffer for it? She thought of Arlo Williams at the seventh-grade picnic taking hours to build up the nerve to put his arm around her.

This guy was so *good* at kissing. She understood what

that meant as she never had before. He was her first real make-out partner, but in the distant part of her brain—the place where she'd stuck her conscience—she knew that she was not his.

She pushed him away, flushed. She tried to catch her breath. "I have to ask you something, okay?" she said.

He nodded, obviously eager to get back to kissing her. "Anything you want to know."

She paused. "What's your name?"

Ama thought about it all night and made a decision. It was a hard one, but inescapable: grades don't matter when you're dead.

She found Maureen packing up her gear after breakfast. "I can't do it."

Maureen looked up. "What can't you do?"

"The final rappel."

Maureen nodded thoughtfully. "I know you must feel like that."

"I do feel like that. And it's also true." Ama tried to keep the quaver out of her voice.

"It's not, though."

"Maureen, I can't. I know I can't. Really." Ama nervously tapped the clunky toes of her boots together.

Maureen touched her wrist. "Look, hon. I know it's going to be hard for you. I really do. It's going to take more from you than from anyone else on this trip. I understand that. But you can do it. I know you can. And you're going to feel so good about yourself when it's done."

"I'll be dead by then. How can I feel good about myself when I'm dead?"

"You won't be dead. Would I let you die?"

Ama wanted to answer Maureen's encouraging smile, but she couldn't do it. She recognized what a pretty smile she had, though. Maureen was one of those people whose prettiness crept up on you over time, in step with their niceness.

Ama trudged away to pack up her things. She hoped Carly was off making out with somebody or other so she wouldn't have to talk to her while she pulled down their tent.

"I'm glad you talked to me about it," Maureen called to her.

Ama looked over her shoulder. "But it didn't do any good."

"Maybe it did."

Eleven

"**D**o you want to come out with us later?" Megan asked Jo as she reset table eleven for the third time. It was another busy night at the Surfside, fast turnover and good tips. All the servers were in a happy mood.

All except Bryn and Lila, another bus girl, who overheard this invitation with an expression of shock and envy.

"Sure. Thanks," Jo said. She went about her wiping and setting with a burgeoning sense of rightness. She hadn't realized that she minded not being asked to join the postshift parties. None of the bus girls were invited. But now that she had been asked, she felt sorry for Bryn and Lila. And she felt backwardly sorry for herself for every night before this one.

She'd have to call and get permission, but she guessed her mom would go along with it. Her mom had always wanted her to be popular as she herself had been. It was also good, because Jo wouldn't end up kissing Zach between the restaurant and home, as she had done for the last few nights. She'd get a night off and build up her strength to resist the other things he was wanting her to do with him.

"Let's go to the bowling alley. We can dance," Caroline suggested during the makeup, planning, and gossip session in the bathroom just after the shift ended.

"There's a new guy who cards, though," Sheba said. "Let's go to the Midnight Room. I think somebody's playing tonight."

"Brent will try to get us to stop at the arcade," Megan pointed out.

"And you're the one who has to say no," Violet shot back.

Jo snapped her head back and forth, taking in the different opinions, joyful to be included. She hoped she wouldn't get laughed at for not having a fake ID.

Bryn caught her on her way out of the bathroom. "You're so lucky! I can't believe they asked you to go out with them. Seriously. You make me sick." She said the last thing like it was a compliment.

"It's because of Zach," Lila, the other bus girl, said.

Bryn nodded.

Jo went outside to call her mom, and when she turned on her phone, she saw there was a message from an hour and a half or so earlier.

"Get home in a hurry," her mom said on the message. "I've got a surprise here for you."

She called her mother back. "What is it?" she blurted out.

"It's not a what. It's a who."

"Is Grandma there?"

"Noooo . . ." Her mom was obviously trying to be mysterious.

"It's not Dad, is it?" She knew as she said it that it couldn't be, because if it was, her mom would sound guarded and complicated. She wouldn't present it like this.

"No."

"Then who is it?"

"Come home and see."

"Just tell me," Jo whined, feeling deflated. Jo didn't feel like having to go home and see. She'd rather go out to the bowling alley or the arcade or whatever. "It's probably one of your sisters," she said sullenly, feeling guilty as she did.

"It's not. Just come home, would you?" her mother said. She was starting to get tired of her own game. Nothing between them stayed fun for long.

Jo made her excuses to the group of girls spilling out of

the bathroom and trudged home on the road instead of along the ocean as she usually did. She wasn't going out and having fun and she wasn't even going to get kissed. She found herself wishing Zach would pop out from behind a shrub. Where was he tonight, anyway?

Her big surprise, as her mother had promised, was waiting for her on the front deck with big dark eyes and an earnest expression.

"Hi, Polly," Jo said.

"I hope it's okay that I came," Polly said as they sat on facing counters in Jo's kitchen and Jo ate a bowl of Cheerios.

Jo nodded, her mouth full, eyes on her spoon. She'd taken out her contacts and put on her glasses, which was a relief. She'd been wearing her contacts for days. Besides her family, Polly and Ama were the only ones who knew she wore glasses.

"I thought you might need a friend," Polly said solemnly.

I have a friend. I have plenty of friends. I even have a boyfriend, Jo wanted to say. "Why's that?" she said.

Polly looked at her strangely. "Because of your parents."

Jo looked up. "What do you mean?"

Polly looked baffled. "Because of them splitting up." She looked like she was going to cry.

Jo put her spoon down. "Who told you that?"

"Your mom did. Last time I called. I asked her how she was doing, because, you know, she sounded sad."

"She told you?"

"She thought I already knew. She thought you told me."

Jo didn't know which direction to go in. Every direction was uncomfortable and bad and she couldn't push herself in any of them.

Polly had talked to Jo's mother about it. *Jo* didn't even talk to Jo's mother about it. Polly was hurt and didn't understand why Jo hadn't told her.

"It's not that big of a deal," Jo murmured. She looked down at her Cheerios, but she couldn't eat another one.

"It's not?"

Jo shook her head. She felt unimaginably tired all of a sudden. She didn't know if she could make it to her bed.

"You sure you're okay?" Polly was studying her carefully.

Jo got up. "Yeah, just tired," she said. "It was a long shift at the restaurant. My feet are aching."

"You want to just go to bed?" Polly's eyes were forgiving. She could have pressed her own hurt feelings on Jo or demanded the nitty-gritty of exactly what had happened with her parents, but she didn't. She didn't want Jo to feel bad.

"I guess so." Jo did feel bad. In too many ways to think about. She also felt guilty. "Thanks for coming, Pollywog. It was nice of you."

Polly nodded and followed Jo to her bedroom. Jo saw that Polly had already pulled out the trundle bed and found a pillow and blanket for herself. Her suitcase sat next to the dresser. She knew her way around the linen closet. She'd slept here many times.

"Maybe we can go to the beach tomorrow," Polly suggested.

"Okay," Jo said, wondering just how long Polly was planning to stay. Jo felt guilty as she tried to think of nice ways to tell Polly she had to go home.

As they lay in the dark, Jo tried to fall asleep, but tired as she was, she couldn't. She could tell from Polly's breathing that Polly hadn't fallen asleep either. But she was quiet.

"I'm sorry I'm not, you know, up for doing stuff tonight," Jo said.

Polly nodded in the near-darkness. "That's okay. I understand. I know it's a hard time for you."

Dear Polly,
I hate my tent mate, Carly. I hate her. She took my pink bandana without asking, and when I went looking for her, I found her in the woods with guess who? Noah!!! I'm not kidding! I did not stay long enough to see what they were doing,

but I can imagine it. She is the biggest slut ever! The one boy on this trip she hasn't made out with is Andy, and that's only because he hasn't hit puberty yet!

I hate her and I hate Noah. I hate camping and hiking and climbing and my backpack and my tent and my boots.

Love, spite, and bile
from your old friend,
Ama

Dear Papa,

Thank you for your letter. The forests and mountains really are majestic, as you say. You are right that this trip is a great opportunity for me to see and get to know our new country.

Best love to Maman and Bob and Esi.

Love,
Ama

The first letter Ama threw away immediately. She had no intention of sending it. She needed to vent and Polly was always the one for that, the best and least judgmental listener. The second letter she put in the bag for the mail drop in Port Angeles.

When Jo first woke, she didn't know where she was. She was scared and disoriented for a moment, thinking she was home in Bethesda and Finn was calling to her from his bedroom next to hers. She could hear his voice perfectly, even though she hadn't heard it for such a long time. Her heart was racing as she sat up in her bed. Slowly she focused her eyes on her surroundings. Sunshine was spilling through the window. She heard the roll of the waves beyond the house. Gradually she placed herself in space and time. It wasn't always a relief to remember where you were.

"Are you okay?" Polly asked, stepping into her room from the hallway, looking worried. "You were shouting."

Jo nodded. "I'm fine. I was dreaming, I guess," she said, though her heart still pounded. She saw that Polly was dressed and alert, a book in her hand. Jo rubbed her eyes. "What time is it?"

"Noon."

"Really?"

"Yeah."

"I didn't mean to sleep so late," Jo said.

"That's all right. Do you want to go to the beach?"

"Okay," she said. "I'll get ready." Polly took up her toiletry kit and disappeared into the guest bathroom, leaving Jo hers to use. Jo wondered about the suitcase. She wondered again how long Polly intended to stay.

Jo put on a bathing suit and threw some stuff in a bag. Polly was ready and waiting at the door.

She realized, as they walked along, how pale Polly was and also how small her arms looked. She looked like a moon moth, out of place in the sunshine. Did Polly go outside ever? Did she have any life at all? Jo felt a pang at that thought, but she resisted it. Was it really Jo's job to have to worry about Polly forever?

On the wide sand beach they laid out towels together, slathered on sunscreen—with Jo's orange-yellow hair she was prone to sunburn and freckles—and lay there until they got hot. Then they jumped into the ocean.

The waves were big and got bigger. They jumped and dove in unison. Polly got clobbered by a wave and stood up, laughing. She was remarkably strong and sturdy for a moon moth. When Jo leapt for a wave but lost her feet in the current, Polly reached out for her hand. Jo took it but then she dropped it, because of the guilt and all the unspoken things.

After that they lay back on the towels and let the sun dry them.

"How's your dad handling it?" Polly asked after a silence.

Jo squeezed her eyes shut against the sun. "Handling what?" she said.

Polly rolled onto her side to look at Jo.

"You mean him and my mom splitting up," Jo said, only half obligingly.

Polly nodded, staring into Jo with her big, serious eyes.

Jo fiddled with the strap of her bathing suit and looked away.

"It seems like it's been really hard for them since Finn, you know?" Polly asked.

At that moment, Jo saw a group of her restaurant friends walking in a loose cluster toward her across the glowing sand. At the back of the group she saw Zach, godlike in his blue surf trunks.

"Hey, Goldie," Megan shouted, waving.

Jo sat up. "Hey." She waved to the group. The sun sparked off the ocean into her eyes. Most of them she knew, but a couple of the girls were unfamiliar. "How's it going?"

Megan looked at Polly questioningly.

Jo took in Polly's childish bathing suit and her weird hat and her buckteeth as she squinted into the sun. Jo saw Polly through Megan's eyes, and it didn't look good. Jo felt guilty, but she wished she could make it seem that she and Polly didn't know each other, even though they were lying side by side on towels. "This is, uh, Polly," Jo said.

Megan nodded.

"Hi," said Polly.

"We're going to play volleyball up by Oak Street if you want to come."

"Okay, thanks. Maybe we'll come by," Jo said. There was no way she was bringing Polly to play volleyball with them.

Zach lagged a little behind the rest of the group. He gave her a long look, taking in every bit of her that wasn't covered by her lavender and white striped bikini. He winked at her.

"See you tonight, Goldie," he called before he caught up with the rest of them.

As they walked away Jo found herself wishing she was going with them. They didn't know her parents and they hadn't known Finn, and the big relief was that they probably didn't care.

"Who's Goldie?" Polly said after they had gone.

Jo shrugged and started to make a hill of sand. "That's what they call me at work."

When the doorbell rang through the big, airy glass beach house, Polly followed Jo to get it. She immediately recognized the girl at the door from school. She recognized her tiny features and squinty blue eyes and sullen mouth, but she couldn't remember her name.

"You know Bryn, right?" Jo asked, ushering Bryn into the house.

"Yeah. From school," Polly said. She began chewing on her thumbnail. Bryn did not look pleased to see her. Polly knew she was not Bryn's kind of person. Bryn was one of the girls Jo had started hanging out with at the end of seventh grade, and Polly could not figure out why.

"Do you guys want some lemonade?" Polly asked. It was obvious Bryn was very eager to talk to Jo about something and she didn't want to do it with Polly around.

Polly took her time with the lemonade. She wondered if Jo's mom was out in the back. She felt like Jo's mom was acting more like her friend than Jo was.

Polly heard their voices coming from Jo's room, so she carefully carried the three glasses down the hallway. Her steps slowed as she heard what Bryn was saying. She didn't mean to, but Bryn's voice was grainy and insistent, and Polly's ears were unusually sensitive.

"You didn't go?" Bryn's voice demanded. "You must be joking."

Jo said something, but Polly didn't hear it clearly.

"Because of *her*? You can't be serious. I know you guys used to hang out, but I didn't realize she was still, like, your BFF." Bryn sounded like she was laughing.

Polly didn't hear any response from Jo.

"Seriously, Jo, she's gotta be, like, the weirdest kid at school."

Polly didn't want to take another step forward, but she

couldn't make herself back away. It seemed pretty clear that Bryn was talking about her.

"Anyway, what is she doing here?" Bryn demanded to Jo's inaudible response.

The lemonade sloshed a little in the glasses as Polly's hands shook. She didn't want to be heard. She didn't even want to be there. She couldn't go forward or back.

She waited for Jo to stand up for her. Maybe Polly and Jo weren't as close anymore, and maybe Jo chose to spend more time with kids like Bryn. But Jo and Polly were real friends. You couldn't take that away.

"I didn't invite her. She just came. I wish she'd leave." Jo's words stabbed like individual blades into Polly's ears.

"She's here and you're saying you aren't even friends with her?"

Polly heard nothing, and then Jo's response: "We used to be friends."

Jo heard the thump and crash and rush of footsteps down the hallway. She ran out of her room, past two broken glasses and a spreading puddle of liquid, and into the kitchen.

Polly stood in the kitchen with a wad of paper towels in her hand and tears on her cheeks. She hurried past Jo to the mess in the hallway. She knelt down, clumsily picking the glass pieces out of the lemonade and laying down the paper towels.

Jo watched her, paralyzed. "Polly, what happened?" she asked, even though she knew. She knew what had happened.

"I broke the glasses," Polly said to the floor. Jo heard the sob in Polly's voice and she knelt down too and began to pick up bits of glass.

"Polly—"

Polly gathered the soaked paper towels and carried them to the kitchen garbage. She dumped them, along with the pieces of glass. She went into Jo's room, past Bryn, who sat on the bed flipping through a magazine, and got her suitcase. Jo watched, holding bits of glass in her hands.

Jo stood up and felt dizzy. She felt like there was a strange pressure from above and around her, and it would crumple her legs and send her sprawling.

She followed Polly to the front door. Polly walked out of it, carrying her suitcase, her damp beach towel flapping over her shoulder. Her dark clothes and tall socks looked strange against the dunes. Jo followed a few steps down the path, her feet bare, still holding the pieces of broken glass. Then she stopped and watched Polly walk down the beach, getting smaller as she went.

Jo wanted so badly to feel relieved at seeing Polly

go. She wanted to forget about what had happened. Jo wanted to tell herself that Polly hadn't really heard much of anything, and she wanted herself to believe it. She wanted to go back into the house and laugh about it with Bryn, but she couldn't move.

For two years, Jo had instinctively kept her old friends separate from her new ones. She had dreaded having Polly and Bryn in the same place, and not just because Polly would embarrass her. The deeper dread was that she, Jo, would be cruel.

Jo looked down at her hands and saw that they were bleeding.

Twelve

"**P**olly, what's the matter? How come you're not eating anything?"

Polly drew her eyes up from her take-out Thai noodles
and focused them on Dia. "I'm just . . . not that hungry."

"Did you eat a late lunch?"

Polly thought back to lunch. Had she eaten lunch? She
shrugged.

"Did you have a bad day?"

Polly had done little eating or speaking since she'd returned from Rehoboth Beach, but Dia was just starting to
notice. Polly thought back on her day. Had she had a bad
day? She shrugged again.

"What did you do this afternoon?" Dia was clearly in a

141

fine mood. She was drinking some kind of whiskey cock-
tail with lemonade and maraschino cherries.

"Regular stuff. I read."

Dia nodded. She was staring purposefully at Polly. "Did
you have a bad time with Jo at the beach?"

Dia didn't notice stuff often, but when she did she was
smart.

Polly shrugged again.

"What happened?"

Polly considered her mother's short, inky hair and the
glint of the gold stud in the side of her nose.

What would Jo's friend Bryn think of Dia? Could Bryn
think of a bigger word than *weird*? Probably not. To a person like Bryn the world was amazingly simple. You were
either normal or weird. Normal was a small and rigid category and weird was a much bigger but also rigid category.
It didn't matter how you were weird or why you were
weird. There was no diversity in weird. There were no de-
grees of weird. You just were or you weren't. Those were
the possibilities and there weren't any others.

Polly pictured Jo in fourth grade dressed up as Pippi
Longstocking for Halloween, balancing the giant horse
she'd made out of papier-mâché. She pictured Jo playing
the violin to her tree. Could Jo really stay inside the limits
of normal? Did she really want to?

"She's got a lot of new friends at the beach," Polly said. "Kids who work at the restaurant and on the boardwalk."

Dia nodded knowingly. "And you didn't feel like you fit in?"

Polly knew this was a favorite and familiar tune for Dia. Dia had made a life out of not fitting in. *I'll show you weird,* her mother seemed to say with her clothes and her hair and her sculptures.

Polly shook her head.

"Well, don't lose sleep over the new friends." Dia waved the stem of a maraschino cherry. "Girls like us are a hell of a lot more interesting. Trust me on that."

Polly nodded, but she wasn't sure she wanted to be a girl "like us." She didn't want to be interesting. Maybe it was okay when you were grown up and you were in control of it, but being interesting in high school was no fun at all.

Polly wondered what could happen if she lost a few more pounds and got started as a model. What if she had a real head shot, the kind they promised you at the end of modeling camp? What if she actually got hired for a job?

What if Bryn saw Polly in a magazine? What if Jo saw it? What if they knew that her grandmother had been a real model, a famous one? What would they think then?

Dia got up and fixed herself another drink. When she sat

back down she looked solemn. "I have to say, Polly, I'm kind of surprised at Jo, though. And I guess Ama, too."

"What do you mean?" Polly asked.

"Lots of friendships fall apart when you get to be teenagers," Dia said, sighing philosophically. "Kids get so narrow-minded in high school. I guess that's pretty typical. But I thought you three promised more."

I thought we did too, Polly thought.

"Aunt Candice wants me to zip up to Baltimore for a night or two to meet her new boyfriend," Jo's mother told her the next afternoon.

Jo nodded. Aunt Candice was a few years ahead of her mom in the divorce process. She was already having boyfriends. She made for a weird kind of role model, Jo thought.

"Are you going to go?" Jo said.

"I'd like to." Her mom looked happier than she had in a while. "He's a musician. He's playing a set on Friday night."

The way her mother said it, the single thing that her life had been missing for the last ten years was a musician playing a set in Baltimore on Friday night.

"That's fine. I don't mind." The gears in Jo's brain started to turn.

"You could stay next door," her mother said hopefully. "Jeannie said she'd be delighted to have you."

Jeannie next door had twin four-year-old boys. Jo knew she'd spend any free time there babysitting. But if she stayed here . . . well, there was Zach. There were Bryn and the group at the restaurant. There was no curfew. There were endless intriguing possibilities.

"I can stay here," Jo said. "It's fine. Jeannie's right next door if I need anything."

Her mother looked uncertain. She wanted this to work. She didn't want to run into any obstruction from Jo, and Jo knew it.

"Seriously, Mom. It's no problem. We've got Jeannie on one side and Mrs. Gluck on the other. She never goes anywhere."

Her mom nodded slowly. "Do you really think you'd be all right?"

"Of course. You'll have your phone, I'll have mine. You'll only be a couple hours away. I won't use the stove. What could happen?"

Her mom really wanted to go. "Well. Maybe. I don't know. Do you think you should talk to your dad about it?"

Jo breathed out in impatience. "Mom, do you really think Dad would care?"

Gia was one of the earliest supermodels and probably the most tragic, Polly concluded after extensive research on-line. Cindy Crawford was one of Polly's favorites because she had been her high school's valedictorian and studied engineering at Northwestern University.

Polly stood up from her computer and wandered into the bathroom. She climbed up onto the sink to take a look at her backside in the tall mirror. Had it gotten any smaller? According to the digital scale at Wallman's drugstore yesterday, she'd lost six and a half pounds.

Polly thought about her research. She especially liked Iman, because Iman was from Africa, like Ama. In fact, Iman looked like Ama, or at least the way Polly imagined Ama would look when she got older. Christy Turlington practiced yoga, which Polly respected, and Heidi Klum had a good head for business and had started her own TV show.

Polly turned to look at herself from the front. She was getting pretty good at dieting, she realized. She was pretty pleased with herself for that. A lot of the models she'd been reading about took diet pills or illegal drugs or smoked cigarettes to stay thin. Polly was glad she wouldn't have to resort to those measures.

One thing that made it easier was that Polly ate a lot of her meals by herself, so if she skipped them, no one really noticed. She pictured Ama's family around the dinner table every night. There was no way you could skip dinner if you were Ama. Not that Ama wanted to skip any dinners. Unlike Polly, Ama was naturally thin to begin with.

Polly had hoped to lose three and a half more pounds before she went to camp, but she'd read an article online that said that you could stunt your growth if you didn't eat enough. Was it more important to be thin or tall?

Kate Moss was harder to warm up to, Polly found. She was the current subject of Polly's research. You couldn't do a thorough study of models without Kate Moss, and though Kate Moss was exceptionally beautiful she was also the mother of a young daughter. When Polly looked at the pictures online of Kate Moss partying with crazy, druggy rock stars, she couldn't help thinking of the daughter.

Polly's stomach looked flat and her waist was small, but her hips and butt looked no different. Her face was thinner and her cheekbones stuck out more, but her bra fit just the same.

When she went into her room to get dressed, she still felt ungainly in her jean shorts. She still stooped self-consciously in her tank top. She still suffered the same old frustration at Dia for not coming home when she said she would. She still replayed the words that Jo had said to Bryn in Rehoboth Beach, as hard as she tried not to.

Polly was pretty good at dieting, all right, but she was beginning to wonder whether you ever lost the parts of yourself you wanted to lose.

● ● ●

"I totally love those socks," Carly gushed. "Do they have the separate toes? I had some like that once, but the dryer ate one of them."

Ama nodded grimly at Carly as they reassembled their tent two nights later.

"I'm always buying new socks, aren't you?" Carly nattered on. "For a while I stopped wearing them, but my running shoes really started to stink." Carly laughed at her own hilarity, and Ama used what weight she had to drive a corner post into the ground.

"Then I decided to get all the same kind, so it doesn't matter if you lose one, you know?"

Ama didn't know. Ama's mother washed clothes with such care that she almost never lost their socks. But Ama remained silent. It didn't seem to bother Carly, nor did she even seem to notice that Ama wasn't answering her and hadn't answered her in three days, since the episode with Noah.

When Ama next looked up, the tent was done. As much as Carly talked, she was a remarkably efficient tent assembler.

"I'm starving," Carly declared, heading off to join the dinner-making team.

Ama wandered around alone, examining the anthills on either side of her. She'd become well versed in ants, both red and black, and did a good job of not setting up their tent on top of any.

She didn't want to join the dinner group, because she didn't want to watch Carly flirting with Noah again. She'd spent too much time over the last three days obsessing about whether Carly and Noah were sneaking off together, and also avoiding any opportunity to find out.

Did Carly need to have *all* the boys? Every last one? Could she leave one for anyone else?

What if she did leave one for me? Ama asked herself fitfully. *What would I do about it? Would I talk to him? Would I sit next to him? Would I even stay put for two minutes when he sat next to me?* Nothing, no, no, and no. Why shouldn't Carly have Noah, too? Carly had enough for all of them, whereas Ama didn't have anything for anyone.

That night was cold. Ama lay shivering in her sleeping bag, alternating between fretting about the rappel and fretting about Carly and Noah. This was interrupted when Carly arrived at the entrance to the tent.

Ama immediately pretended to be asleep so she wouldn't have to talk to her, and again it was a miscalculation. Like she had on that first night, Carly brought a guest.

Was it Noah? Ama couldn't move. She opened one eye for a fraction of a second and saw the dark, straight hair. It was Noah! She waited to hear his voice as the two of them crowded into the little tent. She didn't dare turn her head.

Was it definitely him? He didn't say anything. In mortification she listened to Carly's whispers and giggles. And then she listened to the unmistakable sound of kissing.

This was too much! She couldn't take it.

In a fit of anger and jealousy mixed with a few parts humiliation, Ama gathered her sleeping bag around herself and unzipped the entrance with hurried, shaking hands. She grabbed her pack and crashed out of the tent. She tried to walk in her sleeping bag, but she couldn't. She stumbled and tripped, dropped her pack, and clumsily fought for her balance.

"Oops. I guess she wasn't asleep," she heard Carly say from inside the tent.

"I guess not," the boy—Noah?—answered.

They whispered and laughed and Ama needed desperately to get away. She couldn't stay there for as long as it would take to get out of her sleeping bag, so she started hopping. It was a hard combination, anger and hopping. She felt ridiculous. But it was impossible, she knew, to feel more ridiculous than she looked.

She hopped to the edge of the campsite. She wanted to make a statement with her anger. She heard a far-off animal sound. But not *that* big a statement. She didn't want to die.

She slumped over and thought for a moment. She carefully stowed her pack under a clump of dense shrubbery so her stuff wouldn't get too wet if it rained in the night. She stretched out and nestled down, down into her sleeping bag so her head was all the way in.

It was like her own little tiny tent, with no slutty tent mates and no disappointing boys in it. *I love you, sleeping bag,* she thought. Who needed boys or good grades or even self-respect when you had your own little tiny tent? Maybe she had been born a tortoise in another life.

If I never came out, I think I might be happy, she told herself. She imagined there were rooms and corridors down in her sleeping bag and lots of objects to keep her company. She was like Oscar the Grouch on *Sesame Street,* whom she used to watch sometimes in Ghana. Space magically released Oscar from its normal rules and allowed him to have lots of room and plenty of objects inside his little aluminum garbage can. Maybe that was how her sleeping bag could be.

And with that in her mind, Ama's thoughts went along in their pretty unweaving toward sleep.

It is said that
the sound of wind through
willow trees is the
whispering of fairies into
the poet's ear.

It is also said that
the willow can
uproot itself, stalk
travelers, and
mutter at them.

Thirteen

"I could change it. I don't mind," Polly said to Ms. Miller, the hair and makeup teacher at modeling camp, who stood shaking her head at Polly's hair.

"I'm thinking extensions," the woman said. "What about the color?"

Polly peered at herself in the mirror. "What about it?"

"It's natural?"

"Um. Yes."

"It's so severe. So dark."

"I could lighten it?" Polly said tentatively. She wondered what her mother would have to say about that. Her mother was all for hair dye, but only if it was black or pink or green or blue. Blond would not sit well with Dia. As Polly looked around the class, she recognized that she was both the oldest and by far the least blond. Probably not all of the girls came that way naturally.

That was one thing that surprised Polly about modeling camp. Although the brochure said ages nine to sixteen, Polly, at fourteen, was fully two years older than the next-oldest camper.

Another thing was that the camp was situated right near the parking lot of a large shopping mall, and it turned out that the curriculum involved a lot of supervised shopping. Polly had not been expecting woods on a lake and tents and canoes, exactly, but she hadn't been expecting a parking lot and a mall, either.

The shopping was a problem for one thing because she didn't like shopping and for another thing because she had spent every dollar she had earned babysitting on getting to the camp in the first place. That didn't leave any budget for shopping or the camp snack bar. Which was probably just as well, because she still had two pounds to lose.

Which led her to another of the things she was surprised about. For a bunch of girls who aspired to be models, they sure did spend a lot of time in the snack bar.

During the free periods in the middle of the day, while the other girls sat in the snack bar and watched TV, Polly sat in the classroom and continued her research on famous models. She knew she should be making more of an effort to get some friends, but she was self-conscious about being older and she knew she was different.

Anyway, it was easier for her to spend time among supermodels rather than with actual girls who only hoped for the things the supermodels already had, and with whom the conversation was supposed to go both ways.

Jo put on her favorite shorts and wore her hair down for her shift that night, hoping to make herself feel better. She wanted badly to see Zach. When she saw him all her regular, slow thoughts retreated and new, darting thoughts took over, and today that seemed like it would be a good thing.

When she spotted him in the dining area, she went over to him and put her hand briefly in his back pocket. "Hi, Zach."

She wanted him to kiss her, just a tiny one. That was the one thing she had been focusing on for the last twelve hours, but he was rushing to the kitchen to put in his first order.

Zach, Zach, Zach, Zach, Zach. Now that she knew his name she did enjoy saying it. *Are you my boyfriend? Are you, Zach, my boyfriend?*

During her break, she hung out in the back with the other girls as they smoked and text-messaged, their fingers a blur. She felt like she was one of them now, minus the cigarettes. Jo recognized a new girl she'd spotted several times over the course of the night.

"Is this your first shift?" Jo asked her.

"This summer, yeah," the girl said. "I worked here last August."

She was probably seventeen or eighteen, Jo guessed, but she looked older. She wore the standard-issue Surfside T-shirt, but she filled it out in a way that Jo did not. She had luxurious dark hair, good tanning skin, and a substantial nose. She was striking, more sexy than pretty.

"I'm Jo," Jo said. "Are you from D.C.?"

"Bethesda. What about you?"

"Same," Jo said. "Where do you go to school?"

"South Bethesda. I'm a senior."

Jo nodded, feeling very young and small. She decided not to say that was where she went too. She wanted this girl to see her as a fellow waitress (sort of) with a boyfriend, and not as just a measly high school freshman.

"Are you bussing?" the girl asked somewhat dismissively, looking around in her purse for something.

"Yeah," Jo said. She wanted this girl to know that she wasn't just some little hanger-on, that she was part of the group. She was the girlfriend of the hands-down hottest guy in the place. She was a busser, yes, but she had stature here, even with the waiters.

The girl applied some gloss to her lips, swung her purse over her shoulder, and headed back into the restaurant.

"Hey, Effie, hold up," Violet called after her.

Jo, feeling pale and extra-freckly, walked back to the dishwashing station with as much dignity as possible. She thought about the night ahead. When Zach popped up at the end of the shift, as he inevitably would, and wanted to take her down to the beach and kiss her, she would go for it. Not like she hadn't before, but this time would be different. She was ready to have a real boyfriend now. She knew the value of a guy like Zach, and she didn't want to mess it up.

By ten-fifteen all but one party of diners had left and Jo was cleaning and setting up tables for the following day. She looked around to catch Zach's eye, but he wasn't anywhere in the dining area.

Bryn wheeled the silverware cart over. "I heard Zach's girlfriend from last summer is back," she announced in a stage whisper.

"What are you talking about?"

"That new waitress? You know, the one with the huge boobs and the dark hair? She told Megan that Zach is her boyfriend. They hooked up last summer and stayed together all year."

Not very close together, Jo thought, but did not say. She

kept setting the table, like this was of no special interest to her. "I don't believe it. Megan told you that?"

"Violet told me. Megan told Violet."

"Right," Jo said, casually, as though she didn't much believe it or care.

Jo looked around in mounting frustration. She had seven tables still to set and one party that would not leave. It was unfair, because most of the waiters were allowed to go once their section had cleared out, while the bussers had to stay until every last table in their section was wiped and set.

The majority of the girls were already gathered in the bathroom. Earlier, during the lunch shift, Megan had said Jo could come along tonight, but Jo knew they weren't all going to wait for her. They would take off for the night's activities while Jo was still stuck here. Zach would wait for her, though.

She wiped manically, ignoring Bryn and her gossip. The big-boobed, dark-haired girl might believe she was Zach's girlfriend, but she was obviously wrong. Zach didn't think so. Maybe they had hooked up last summer. That was totally possible. But Zach had clearly moved on, and that girl was just going to have to deal with it.

Jo watched with a sense of desperation as the girls left in a noisy group. The other waiters had mostly closed out too. She was left among the lowly people: Brownie, Jordan-the-doofus, and Carlos. Even Bryn and Lila had already left.

She and Brownie wrapped up the paper from table after table with all the crab shells and guts in them and carried them to the big garbage cans out back. Jo was going too fast to be careful. She was going to stink of crab guts for the rest of her life.

Zach was probably waiting out back for her. He'd jump out from behind a Dumpster or something. But how long would he wait?

She considered leaving. Would Jordan fire her? He'd have to give her at least one more chance, wouldn't he?

When she finally got out of the restaurant Zach was gone. The rest of the group was long gone.

She took out her cell phone to call her mom. She couldn't just go home. No possible way.

"Mom, I'm going to go out with the staff for like, half an hour, okay?"

"Jo, it's almost eleven."

"I'll be back by eleven-twenty at the latest. I promise."

"Do you want me to come pick you up?"

"No, that's okay. I'm fine."

"Honey, did you call your dad?"

Damn. She was supposed to call him and she forgot, just like she forgot last night and the night before. "It was really busy. I'll call tomorrow."

She walked fast along the boardwalk, hoping the guilt wouldn't get a chance to settle on her. She appreciated the fast-blowing wind against her face.

She'd pass by the big arcade and then swing past the Chatterbox. There weren't that many places they could be, unless they were partying on the beach.

They weren't in the arcade, but she did recognize some familiar faces as she approached the Chatterbox. The group of them liked to sit at the big table by the front window. She grabbed the brass door handle and was about to pull it open and walk in when she caught sight of Zach through the big window.

She felt her hands shaking as she dropped them to her sides and backed away from the light.

She'd really only seen half of Zach's face, because the other half was buried in the neck of the dark-haired girl. The girl had her arm looped around him possessively while she talked to somebody across the table.

The dark-haired girl thought Zach was her boyfriend, and Zach apparently agreed.

Ama dreamed rough dreams that night, both tedious and strenuous. She went in and out of sleep, too tired to keep track of anything.

The first sting came after dawn. She coiled and scratched her ankle and threaded it into the narrative of her dream.

Some time later, the second and third stings came, dream-like too, but when the fifth through the fiftieth came all at once, she had no choice but to wake up and stick her head out the top of her sleeping bag and scream.

She stripped off her sleeping bag and smacked at her ankles and arms.

Fire ants! Ahhhhhhh! She jumped around and screamed and slapped with superhuman speed and dexterity until she got them all off.

After that she looked up slowly, very slowly. In the full light of day she looked up, expecting to see the rest of the campers watching her insane performance.

But there wasn't anyone around. She was disoriented. She felt the sun on her head. It was later than she'd thought.

She turned around and saw the grassy hill behind her. When she'd fallen asleep she'd been at the edge of the campsite, and now she wasn't.

She must have rolled down the hill. Amazing but true. She saw the bushes where she'd left her pack, uphill and several yards away.

She lifted her sleeping bag and wrapped it around her shoulders. So much for its magical powers of protection. She headed slowly up the hill.

She found her backpack right away, just where she'd left it. She pulled it from the bushes and walked into the campsite. At first, she was relieved that it was empty so nobody could make fun of her for being attacked by vicious ants and rolling down a hill in her sleep. But that relief was short-lived. Where was everybody?

She walked around the clearing. She saw where they'd had their fire, and a few remnants from cooking. This was indeed the campsite. She hadn't woken up in an alternate universe or anything.

She tried to remember the plan for today. They were going to hike down into a canyon, she recalled. They were supposed to get an early start, probably hiking the first hour before sunrise.

The worry was alive and churning in her intestines, growing by the minute. Had they left her? How could that have happened? Wouldn't they notice she wasn't there? She thought of how often she'd lagged behind the rest of the group. Hadn't they seen her pack? She thought of how she'd carefully buried it in the bushes.

"Hello?" she called out. Her voice sounded timid and small in the forest. "Hello?" she tried more loudly.

Maybe if she started hiking she could catch up with them? She tried to push aside the knowledge that she could barely catch up with them even when she got a head start. Which direction had they gone in?

The canyon had to be downhill, she thought. Canyons were made from water. Water traveled down. Her thoughts raced up and down and around. They couldn't have gone in the direction she had rolled in, because if they'd gone that way, they would have seen her.

In a panic she began stuffing her sleeping bag into her pack. She strode several yards before she realized she hadn't gotten dressed. She wildly unpacked the top of her pack and pulled on the first clothes she saw over her long underwear.

She marched along, downhill, trying to quiet the panic. She walked faster and faster. What if she couldn't find them? What if she wandered around lost, without food or water? She could die here and nobody would even notice!

She scanned the trees for markings of a trail, but saw none. Just trees and trees and trees and they were all the same. *What should I do?*

"Hello?" she shouted uselessly at the trees.

She sped up her pace to a near run, vaguely recognizing how much stronger her legs had gotten, how much sturdier her ankles were. She kept on going, barely noticing that she was out of breath and her lungs were aching. She barely felt the weight of her pack.

"Hello?" she shouted down a hill an hour or more later, searching for signs of water, hearing nobody.

Fourteen

"Can I ask you something?" Jo had gotten to the restaurant early so she could catch Zach on his way in.

Zach glanced around and then at his cell phone, which he held in his hand. "Anything you want to know," he said lightly, but he didn't look quite like he meant it. "Until my shift starts in three minutes."

"Do you have a girlfriend?" She'd debated the wording of it for all the hours it had taken her to fall asleep the night before, and that was what she had come up with. She'd thought of saying *Do you have* another *girlfriend?* but she was worried about being confusing or presumptuous at such a moment. If he really liked her, he'd say *You're my girlfriend, Goldie.*

"Do I what?" he said, like he was hard of hearing.

"Do you have a girlfriend?" *Besides me?* a part of her wanted to say. *Besides you?* she wanted him to say.

"You mean Effie?" he asked.

That was the wrong answer. "I don't know who I mean. Is Effie your girlfriend? Is she the one with the dark hair and the big—if she is, then I guess that's who I mean." Jo wished her mouth would stop with the talking.

"Effie and I got together when we were working here last summer," he said, jiggling his phone around in his hand. "I didn't realize she was coming back."

I bet you didn't, Jo thought. It might have been the first completely true thing he'd said. "Are you still together?"

He sighed, as though her line of questioning was irrelevant and somewhat exasperating. "Together? I don't know. I mean, we hang out."

"She says you are her boyfriend. Are you?"

He smiled while shaking his head. "Settle down, Clarence Darrow. I don't know what she says. How do I know?"

Jo was getting annoyed too. "Let me put it this way: if I told her you'd been trying to stick your tongue in my mouth for this entire summer, would she have a problem with it?"

Zach pushed his hair around on the top of his head. He'd stopped smiling. "Jo. Come on."

Until that moment she'd actually thought that he thought her name was Goldie.

Hours later, the sun was casting a pink light, and Ama was losing hope. She walked more slowly now, preparing to accept her early, solitary death.

She wished she could find her way back to last night's campsite. It had finally occurred to her, after hours of panicky twists and turns, that when the group noticed she wasn't there, they would logically send somebody back to the campsite to find her—the last known place where the group was intact—and she wouldn't be there. If she had just stayed put, she would probably have been found and would probably not be facing an early, solitary death. But she hadn't. She'd long ago lost her bearings. She no better knew how to get back to the campsite than how to get anywhere else.

It doesn't matter whether I keep walking or not, she told herself. But she kept walking anyway.

She walked until she spotted a slight clearing and a signpost. Her heart surged. She put a hand to her chest to keep it from jumping right out of there. Was the sign a mirage? She stumbled toward it, grabbing on to it with both hands, making sure it was an actual thing with actual mass.

It was a trail map. It showed a hiking trail, of course, but more importantly, it showed a ranger station. Would the station still be open? Would somebody be there?

She printed the map on her brain. She started walking fast, vaguely aware of how easy it had become for her to follow trails. She followed the markings at top speed. The distance disappeared under her boots. If she had any nagging blisters she couldn't feel them.

She exulted at the sight of the wooden structure as she came upon it. She threw her pack down, raced up to the door, and pounded on it.

"Please be there," she begged of the door. She wasn't even sure if she said it out loud or just in her head. "Please, please, please."

The opening of the door startled her so dramatically she staggered into the building. A very tall middle-aged man in a green ranger outfit and hat stood staring at her as she picked herself up and pulled herself together.

"My group left without me. I got lost," she burst out. She wished she could present herself with a little more poise, but she couldn't. She tried to catch her breath.

The ranger, whose name turned out to be Bob, gave her some time to calm down and then asked her the relevant questions. She figured she made at least a little sense in answering them, because he led her to a phone at a desk and pointed at it. "All yours," he said. "I'm going to try to find the number for Wild Adventures."

He went to another part of the building and left her alone sitting at the desk with the old-fashioned phone.

She picked it up with a shaking hand. Her fingers instinctively called home. She pictured her mother and heard her mother's voice. She hoped she could keep from crying until after she'd explained the problem. But her mom didn't answer. Nobody answered. The answering machine picked up. Ama left a halting message, giving the station's number and asking her parents to call back right away.

Where was her mom? What day was it? What time was it? What time was it here? What time was it there? Was it two or three hours' difference between here and home? What state was she in, anyway?

What a strange set of questions for a person who always prided herself on knowing exactly where and when she was. She thought of Esi, with her giant watch that told the time in all twenty-four time zones always around her wrist.

Ama couldn't remember her father's cell phone number. She couldn't remember the number of his dispatcher. These were numbers she kept in the memory of her cell phone rather than in the memory of her head. Her mother didn't have a cell phone, and she was almost always at home. Except for now!

She knew Esi's number by heart. She should call Esi. But what should she say? *I'm lost? I'm an idiot? I got left and forgotten? Nobody even noticed I was missing? I'm the worst camper in the history of Wild Adventures? By the way, they are giving out grades, Es, and I'm getting an F? Remember how you thought I could go to Princeton just like you?*

She called Esi's number. It rang and rang. She hung up without leaving a message. Esi was spending the summer before medical school working in a chemistry lab. Esi always turned off her phone when she was in the lab or in the library, and those were the two places where she almost always was.

Now what?

Ama rested her head on her arm. *No crying yet,* she warned herself.

There were two other numbers she knew by heart. They were numbers that she'd known well before the day she'd gotten her first cell phone.

Ranger Bob came into the room. "Any luck?"

"So far, no one's picking up. Do you know what time it is?" Ama asked.

"Five after four," he said after checking his watch.

"Do you know what day it is?" Ama asked timidly.

Bob smiled at her. "It's Friday, last time I checked."

Ama nodded. She was too embarrassed to ask him what time zone they were in. Maybe her mom and dad and Bob had gone to Aunt Jessie's for dinner. She wasn't their real aunt but an older friend of her mother's from church. "How about you? Any luck?" Ama asked.

"Not yet. They're looking it up for me at the main station." Ranger Bob went back into his office and Ama stared at the phone.

She called the number of the one person, besides her mother, who was almost sure to pick up.

"Hello?" came the voice after the first ring.

"Is this Polly?" Ama asked.

"Ama, is that you?"

"It's me. Yes." Ama felt an ache in her throat. It was strange to hear a voice so familiar to her in deepest backcountry, in the middle of her long, strange ordeal. Ama had almost begun to think she'd made it all up.

"Where are you?"

"I'm . . . I don't know." She could say that to Polly. Though it was more like something Polly would say to her.

"You're on your trip, though, right? Your camping trip?"

"Yeah. I'm in a ranger station. I got separated from my group and then I got lost."

"Oh, no."

Ama felt tears. "Yeah."

"Have you talked to your parents yet?"

"No. They're not home. I left a message."

"Are you okay?" Polly was right there, and that made a difference. Polly always knew how to listen.

Ama took a deep breath and shuddered a little bit. "I think so."

"What are you going to do?"

"I want to go home."

"You mean home home?"

"Yes."

"Now?"

"As soon as I can get out of here."

"Why?"

Ama stopped. "Why? Because I hate this trip. I hate hiking. I hate my group. I hate my hair. I don't want to stay here." You could complain to Polly. She would pretend to forget what you said if you needed her to, whereas a person like Grace always reminded you of the annoying things you did.

"But don't you have to wait until the end of the trip?" Polly asked.

"I don't care anymore. When my parents call back, I'm going to tell them I want to leave now."

Polly was quiet for a moment. "Is it beautiful there, though?"

"I guess. I don't know," Ama said absently. She spent too much time looking at the ground to really know. "If I stay, I have to rappel off the edge of a huge cliff. And I can't do that."

"Why not?"

"*Why not?* Because I'd probably die is one reason. It's terrifying. I hate heights."

"What about Pony Hill?"

Ama paused, surprised and irritated. "What about Pony Hill?"

"You loved it more than anyone."

Ama shook her head in disbelief. That was so like Polly, so completely immature. It was obvious at moments like this that Polly didn't know her at all anymore.

"Polly, this has *less* than nothing to do with Pony Hill," Ama said.

Polly was quiet for another moment and Ama felt queasy with fatigue and displeasure. Why had she bothered to call Polly? Even when they had been really close, Polly belonged at the bottom of the list in an emergency. "Anyway, why do you care if I stay or go?" Ama asked.

"I don't. I just thought . . . you might be sorry if you came home without trying it."

"I would not be sorry," Ama insisted. "I would be happy."

"Okay," Polly said.

"That way at least I can get an incomplete and not an F," Ama muttered.

"What?" Polly asked.

Ama regretted saying that out loud. She felt like she'd let her gears show. It was another thing Polly would surely not understand. "Nothing. Never mind," she said.

"Just think of how far you could see, though," Polly said wistfully.

"How far you could see from where?" Ama said. "What are you talking about?"

"From the cliff."

"I don't want to see far," Ama snapped. "I just want to come home."

Polly's favorite class at modeling camp was The Photographer's Eye. Each day of class she sat listening intently to theories of color and composition, making tiny doodles in the margin of her notebook. Mr. Seaver, also known as Geoff, was her favorite teacher by far. He was young and relaxed. He was slight in build and wore running shoes and paisley shirts. All the other teachers were older women, most of them with frozen faces and pointy shoes and hair too perfect to move.

"Mr. Seaver is gay, you know," one of the girls in the snack bar told Polly, like Polly should care. But she didn't.

Mr. Seaver had noticed her doodles on the first day, and instead of getting mad at her, as most teachers did, he'd held them up to the light and studied them carefully. "Wow," he said. "You're like a little Edward Gorey. Look at these trees. How do you come up with these?"

Polly didn't know who Edward Gorey was and wasn't sure whether that was a good thing or not. She asked him if he'd rather she stopped doodling.

"Oh, no. By no means."

She had worried at first that he was being sarcastic, but each day he checked them over and gave her an extensive critique at the end of class, mostly consisting of praise.

After the second day, he let her stay and draw and talk in his classroom while the rest of the campers went off to the mall.

He'd showed her some of his photographs of landscapes and cityscapes and he explained that he made his living as a commercial photographer and a teacher, but he loved fine art photography.

"Why do you want to be a model?" he'd asked her on the third day.

She'd flicked her first two fingers against the desk. "My grandmother was a model," she'd said.

Geoff had nodded. "Really? How fascinating. Was she successful? What was her name?"

Here came the hard part. "I don't know."

"You don't know her name? Is she still alive?"

"I'm not sure."

"Okay." He'd waited for her to go on.

"She's my father's mother. I don't know my father, so I don't know her. I just know she was a model."

"I see."

That same afternoon, as she was leaving, she'd put something on his desk.

"What's this?" he'd asked.

"It's a research report I did."

"For school?"

"No. Just . . . for fun, I guess."

" 'The Lives of Supermodels,' " he read. He'd flipped through some of its many pages. "You did all this? All these tables and pictures and captions and everything?"

She'd nodded. She'd felt a bit uncertain. She knew she overwhelmed people with her intensity sometimes.

He took it with him when he left the class that afternoon and brought it back with him the next day. She was already sitting in his classroom when he got there. She liked to be early in case they could spend some extra time talking.

"Polly, this is unbelievable."

She'd cocked her head. She'd gotten too many forked compliments in her life not to keep an eye out for them. "You think so?"

"Absolutely, yes. This is like a doctoral dissertation or something. The teachers at your school must be very proud of you."

"Well, sometimes," she'd said. Except for the teachers who taught algebra, Spanish, and Wind Instruments.

"I never knew the lives of the supermodels could be made to seem so gripping. Seriously. It's like reading the lives of the saints, only with worse morals and better hair."

She'd laughed.

Now, on her fifth day, it was the last hour of camp for the week, and he was letting her hang around in his quiet room while he did paperwork. She didn't feel like having to talk about clothes or makeup or watch model-related reality shows on the TV in the snack bar. She'd just rather sit here and watch the fading pink sunlight slide across the floor.

She had been thinking about Ama and it made her sad. She was touched that Ama had called her from her wilderness trip, but she felt like she had said all the wrong things. She wished she could take the conversation back and say all different things. She felt like she was out of practice at being a friend.

Mr. Seaver was also less talkative than normal and a little sad when he flopped her report down on her desk on his way out the door. He shook his head absently and sighed. "Polly, what are we doing here?"

"Here?"

"In this place. At this camp."

She fiddled with the pages. She looked at the image she'd

drawn for the front cover. She thought about Jo and Bryn. "What do you mean?" she asked uneasily, although in truth she had a faraway sense of it. "Don't we like it here?"

She realized she wanted him to answer because she didn't know.

Fifteen

As she waited for her parents to call, Ama stared at a poster that hung in front of her on the rough, knotted wooden wall. It showed a scene of nature: tall, magnificent black pine trees and a painter's palette of wildflowers against a backdrop of murky blue mountains. It was the kind of beautiful place her father had been imagining for her, but not the kind that she had seen.

When at last the phone rang she snatched it.

"Hello?"

"Ama? Are you there?"

It was her mother. Ama thought she'd gained control of her emotions, but when she heard her mother's voice, she realized she hadn't.

"Ama, is everything okay? Where are you?"

Ama didn't want to open her mouth. She didn't think she could be in charge of what came out.

"Ama? *Où es-tu?*" Her mother shifted into French, as she sometimes did when she was rattled.

"I'm here," Ama squeaked. "I'm on the trip."

"*Tout va bien? Qu'-est-ce qui s'est passé? Dis-moi, Ama.*"

"I—I got separated from my group. I'm okay now."

"*Mais tu vas bien?*"

"Yes. I'm okay." Ama felt the tears streaming down her cheeks.

"You've found your group?" Her mom was comforted enough to switch back to English.

"Not yet." Ama wished she had a Kleenex to blow her nose into.

"Not yet? Where are they? Where are you? Your voice sounds strange, Ama."

Ama held the phone away and quietly blew her nose into her sleeve. It was disgusting, but what could she do?

"I—I found a park ranger. He's going to find them for me."

"Do the teachers know where you are?"

"No."

"Oh, Ama. *Chérie.*"

"I got lost. I didn't know where to go." She let herself cry freely. "I hate it here, Maman. I hate this trip. I just want to come home."

"Chérie." Ama's mother was clearly surprised. "I didn't know it was so bad."

"I didn't tell you."

"I'll call the Wild Adventures office right now. I have an emergency number. I'll call you back as soon as I speak to them."

"Okay."

Ama hung up the phone and stared at the poster, and cried. She got lost in the crying. She became so lulled by the rhythm of her sobs she forgot what she was crying about. The phone scared her when it rang again a few minutes later.

It was her father this time. "Ama, you are coming home." Her peaceful father sounded as upset as she had ever heard him.

"Really?" She tried to make her voice steady, but she hiccupped instead.

"The organization is incompetent! Your group leaders do not even know where you are! We are arranging for you to be picked up and taken to the airport. You are coming home. You cannot stay there."

The relief was like a warm tide lapping at her feet. She looked out over its calm, boundless mercy.

"They say the course won't appear on your transcript for credit if you don't complete it, but we can worry about that later."

"That's okay. That's no problem!" Ama practically shouted. She could go home. Her parents were bringing her home. No more hiking. No more blisters. No more Carly. No rappel! God, no rappel! No F! Nothing on her transcript! It was too good!

She sniffled. "Okay."

"Ama, please put the ranger on the phone. We need to speak with an adult."

"But—"

"Please get him."

Ama put the phone down and shuffled toward the other room of the building. She cleared her throat. "Uh, Bob?" she called timidly.

She overheard him talking on another phone. "Excuse me," she said. "I'm sorry to interrupt. But my dad would like to speak with you."

Bob gave some final instructions, hung up, and strode from one phone to the other. "I made contact with the Wild Adventure people," he explained to her en route, just before he picked up and launched into long and complex arrangements with her father.

Ama barely heard the words of the conversation. She sat in a chair by the wall and stared at the nature poster and scratched her head. She felt like a little kid who hadn't learned to talk yet.

After that, Ranger Bob made more phone calls. Ama felt

her head begin to droop and her eyelids fall. Her stomach rumbled.

She dreamed of food at first. In her dream she was in the kitchen at Jo's house, and Polly, with flour all over the front of her favorite cowboy shirt, made Ama pans of brownies and sheets of cookies and tins of fudge with chocolate chips and a pink cake with seven layers, but Ama couldn't have any of it.

"I can't afford it," Ama said, watching in wonderment as the sweet things burst into flowers, pans of tulips and daisies and crawling pink roses spreading through the kitchen.

"But it's free," Polly said.

"Ama?" Ranger Bob broke into Ama's dream. "It's Maureen, your group leader on the phone. She wants to talk to you."

Groggy and disoriented, Ama took the phone.

"Maureen?"

"Ama, hon, I am so, so sorry for what happened today." Maureen sounded like she was going to cry.

Ama breathed out. "That's okay," she mumbled.

"No it's not. It's really not. We left the campsite this morning when it was still dark and we got scattered right away. I didn't see you or your pack, so I figured you'd gone with the first group. As soon as we stopped for a water break, we realized you weren't there. Noah and I ran back to find you, but you must have already left."

Ama nodded, feeling her eyes fill. She should have just stayed where she was at the campsite and waited for them. That had been the obvious thing to do. At the very beginning of the trip, that was what the leaders told them they should do if they ever got lost or separated from the group.

"I feel terrible, Ama. We all do. We've all been worried sick."

"That's okay," Ama said again. Had it really happened just this morning? It seemed so far away.

Ama said good-bye. She was too tired to recount what she had gone through or issue forgiveness.

When she hung up the phone she saw that it was black outside the windows.

"We're going to have you camp here at the station tonight," Bob explained to her kindly. "That seems to make the most sense. Your group is going to pick you up on the bus in the morning. You'll leave the group at their next trailhead and your group leader, Jared, will drive you on to the airport. Your parents are arranging your flight home. They'll be in touch directly with the group leaders once they have it confirmed."

Ama nodded. Nobody was asking her opinion about anything, she noticed. Nobody seemed to need her input.

"Why don't I make you something to eat? Are you hungry?"

Bob made her rice and beans from a bag. She was too hungry and too tired to taste it much. Or maybe it didn't have any taste to taste. She wasn't sure.

"My brother's name is Bob," she told him, by way of dinner conversation.

"Is he Robert?" Bob asked.

"No, just Bob," Ama said.

Ranger Bob nodded and that was about all they had to say.

After dinner Bob explained that he would be sleeping in a small apartment at the back of the little building, and he showed her where she should lay her sleeping bag and also where there was a bathroom she could use.

It registered with her that she was sleeping in a strange place with a strange man. That was potentially a cause for concern, but she didn't feel scared. She felt tired and hopeful. She was going home! She was getting away from this place. She would see her family! She would fix her hair! She pictured the moment of her reunion with her hair products.

And anyway, she trusted Ranger Bob. He was a ranger straight out of central casting. He was tall and deep-voiced and steady. They probably put him in the ads and pamphlets, if they had any. She felt sure he never littered or started forest fires.

Ama yawned and began laying out her sleeping bag. Suddenly she missed her boots. She realized she'd left them by the door, and she felt insecure without them. She lined them up carefully at the foot of her sleeping bag.

As she bid Bob good night and thanked him, she caught sight of the nature poster again.

"Excuse me, Bob." She pointed to the poster. "Where is that place?"

"That place?" He looked at the poster and looked back at her. "It's here."

"He did *what*?" If Jo had wanted to get Bryn's attention, she had definitely succeeded.

Jo switched the phone from one ear to the other. "Yep. He basically had his head down that girl's shirt. I saw them at the Chatterbox."

"You mean Effie?" Bryn demanded.

"Yes. Effie." Jo hated her name. As much as she loved saying *Zach* she hated saying *Effie*.

"Wow. That *sucks*."

"Seriously. Tell me about it."

"Wait, so tell me *exactly* what happened. Tell me *everything*. Was it last night?"

Jo told the story faithfully, but Bryn kept interrupting her with questions, and Jo got tired of the "exactly" and the "everything" of it pretty quickly. It might have been exciting to hear, but it was painful to tell.

"Wow," Bryn said again at the end of it. "I thought he really liked you."

Jo wondered whether she heard sympathy there or whether it was something else.

She was going to say *I thought he did too*, but the words brought tears to her eyes and she wondered how much more she wanted to expose herself to Bryn. She was only grateful that she was telling Bryn this over the phone and not in person. She felt self-protective in a way she didn't remember ever feeling with Polly or Ama. "It's not that bad," she heard herself saying. "Maybe he's just not into commitments."

"It's not *that bad*?" Bryn echoed incredulously. "Zach was basically making out with another girl, totally forgetting you ever existed, and you say it's not that bad?"

Jo wanted to hang up now. She wondered why she had called Bryn in the first place. What was the point of this exercise? Jo dug deep to find some dignity. "Look, Bryn. His old girlfriend from last summer came back. He was psyched to see her. It's not like we're married or anything. It's not like that makes him an ax murderer." Jo hoped the tears were not audible in her voice.

"Not as far as we know," Bryn replied.

Jo would have laughed if she could have. "I'm pretty sure he's just the kind of guy who can't limit himself to one girl. I'm not exactly the poster girl for commitment, you know. I'm not so sure what I'd do if one of my old boyfriends came along." This was pure fabrication, but it made Jo feel better to say it.

"Well, let me ask you this," Bryn shot back. "Do you think he feels as bad as you do right now?"

Jo felt a tear ease down her face and drop onto her hand. She knew the answer to this question, but she didn't say it.

Ama awoke in the ranger station. She brushed her teeth and packed up her things, caught sight of her reflection, and cringed. Her night of sleeping like a tortoise had not helped matters with her hair.

She went out to wait on a bench by the road, as Ranger Bob instructed. By eight-thirty, the road was dusty and the sun was already hot. Ama's skin was beginning to broil, and her hair, grown large and out of control, had begun to catch things. She tried to brush out the dust and debris, but the whole project was hopeless.

It was the wait of shame. For two hours nothing came by. Not even a bug. Ama decided she would have been happy to see an ant.

At last the yellow bus appeared on the horizon like a

second sun, a grimmer, dirtier version. She pictured herself as the group on the bus must now see her, waiting alone on the bench in the withering sunshine, the lost and confused girl with very huge hair. It was hard to imagine feeling any stupider.

In a billow of dust, the bus ground to a stop and the door opened. Maureen, who was driving, squeezed Ama's hand on the way in, but otherwise the group was silent. The noise of Ama's exertions was magnified in her own ears. She dragged her stuff along, her boots clonking down the narrow center aisle. Her face burned from sun exposure and from shame.

There was only one open seat and it was next to Carly. Oh, well. Ama noisily, gracelessly stowed her stuff and sat down. The bus began moving and she kept her burning face and eyes directly ahead of her.

Suddenly she felt something touch her hands. She looked down to see that Carly had placed something in her lap. She glanced sideways at Carly and then back down at her lap.

Sitting there, quietly and unobtrusively, were two brown hair elastics and the mythical travel-sized packet of Kiehl's Creme with Silk Groom.

It is believed that
a willow branch
in your house will
protect you from
evil and sorcery.

Sixteen

"**M**y God, Polly. You've lost weight," her mother said upon meeting her at the Friendship Heights Metro station on the last day of camp. Dia had worked late at the studio for the last three nights, so Polly had barely seen her.

"Just one pound since last week," Polly said.

"Are you sure?"

"I'm sure. You were just used to seeing me," Polly said. And it was true that you could spend weeks living alongside a person and not see them, especially if you happened to be Polly's mother. Polly had once walked around with pinkeye for four days before Dia noticed. Sometimes it took an absence to make a person look.

"I don't know, honey." Her mother looked perturbed. "You shouldn't lose any more weight, all right? You don't look healthy."

Polly nodded, but she didn't really agree. She was happy, in a way, that her mother had finally noticed. She felt a tiny spark of pride that she was good at losing weight when her mother struggled and failed at it. It was so rare to be better than a grown-up at something; Polly would take this thing.

Polly's mother put her arm around her as they walked across the parking lot to the car. Polly felt oddly distant and close at the same time.

She realized she hadn't eaten at all that day. She felt empty and small, and she liked that feeling. You spent your whole childhood getting bigger. You spent the whole time getting carried less, getting held less, until it was never. There was a strange pleasure in getting smaller instead of bigger for once, in feeling like you could also go backward if you needed to.

"I'm going to drop you home and go back to the studio, okay?" her mother said.

"Okay. Hey, Dia?"

"Yeah?" Her mother pulled out of the parking lot. She squinted like she had a headache.

"Do you want me to come to the studio with you? I could draw or read. I won't disturb you at all."

Polly used to do that when she was much younger. She'd

had a playpen there when she was a baby and a desk with all her drawing things later on. She'd had a little cot where she napped sometimes, and where her mother sometimes sketched her while she slept. The studio had been packed full of sculptures and photographs and wood and clay and piles of things her mother had found on the street, sketches she had taped to the walls, stacks of food, and the odd withered houseplant.

When Polly was six Dia had done the sculpture for which she'd won a big national award. It was cast in bronze and put in the plaza in front of a building downtown, with a plaque in front of it. After that Dia had been asked by a gallery in New York City to show her work and had been given lots of important commissions.

Over time, her mother had gotten backed up in her work and had ended up not finishing most of the commissions. She'd postponed her gallery show year after year. Polly often thought Dia had been happier as an unsuccessful artist than she was as a successful one.

"Oh, Polly." Her mom took her hand off the steering wheel to drink her iced coffee, but she kept her eyes on the road. "Not today. I've got to really concentrate today. But soon. Okay?"

They drove quietly through Bethesda and made the turn onto Solomon Street.

"Hey, Dia?"

"Yeah?"

"There's this modeling and talent convention in New York City next month. All the girls at camp were talking about it. I really want to go."

Dia raised her eyebrows but didn't look over. "In New York?"

"It's three nights. The big scouts from all around the country come for it. You have to get accepted, and I might not. But I sent in my application just in case."

"Let me guess—they accept you so you can pay them hundreds of dollars?" Dia muttered. "Polly, you are getting carried away with all this. I don't know what's gotten into you. You're losing weight and obsessing over all this modeling stuff. You've never been like this before. I don't get it."

Dia was wrong. Polly had been like this before. She was a girl of serial passions: butterflies, papier-mâché, pirates, the novels of Philip Pullman. She'd had many, just not this one, before.

"I'm just interested in it, okay? I want to see if I could be any good at it."

Dia pulled the car up in front of the house and turned to Polly. "What's there to be good at? You just stand around trying to look a certain way. I think there's better use for your talents. I really do."

Polly picked at the stitching on her seat. "If I get in, I really want to go."

Dia tapped the steering wheel. Polly knew she was eager to get going. "It would be expensive. Someone would need to go with you. No, Polly. I don't see how it would work."

"Please, Dia?"

Her mother let out her breath. "I don't think it's a good idea."

But she didn't say no, and Polly got out of the car, shut the door, and strode up the walk with her hopes undiminished.

Because Dia was tired. Not just for today, but for all the days. Because sticking to *no* took a lot more energy than saying yes. That was the factor Polly counted on again and again. Because her mother had little will, and Polly had almost nothing else.

The campsite had a sense of calm the next evening. Ama herself felt subdued as she worked alongside her group members. They had gotten so efficient at dividing up jobs and assembling dinner that they hardly needed to talk. The pasta with tomato sauce tasted uncommonly good. Now that Ama knew she was leaving, she felt she could relax. When Noah tried to steal her chocolate chip cookie, she laughed and fought back. She played along a little, even though he was kind of a jerk.

After dinner, Ama felt quiet and thoughtful. She wandered to the edge of the campsite and perched on a smooth rock overlooking the valley below. The sky was rippled with bands of pink and orange as the round red sun dipped into the mountains. It seemed to her the first sunset she'd seen in a long time.

When Polly had mentioned Pony Hill to her on the phone, it had seemed like a joke to Ama, and it had filled her with indignation. Was it even called Pony Hill? Was that its official name, or was that just what they called it? Even so, she kept thinking about it. She pulled her sleeves over her hands for warmth and tried to remember what she had loved about it.

She had liked running down it, feeling her body getting ahead of her legs, her legs moving more by gravity than effort, feeling a little bit out of control. When they used to visit their trees after school they would always arrive at the top of the hill and look down at the little woods below. You had to run down Pony Hill to get to the trees. It was too steep to walk. Sometimes she and Jo and Polly would hold hands and go as fast as they could, pulling each other and screaming. Sometimes they made it to the bottom still standing on their legs, but more often they ended up rolling down the last part of it. She remembered picking bits of grass and dried leaves out of her pants and shirt and socks and hair. Sometimes they rolled on their sides from the top to the bottom, trying to keep their legs straight and their arms tightly at their sides but usually unraveling along the way. In winter when there was snow, they slid to the bottom on the backs of their down jackets, usually headfirst. On weekends they brought out Jo's sled.

Ama had loved how fast you could go. She loved the feeling it gave you in the bottom of your stomach. And the grass was soft or the snow was soft, so you never hurt yourself. She'd liked the view from the top of the hill. She'd liked trying to pick out their trees in the woods beyond, even though you couldn't really see them from up there.

Ama put her chin on her hand and felt her joints softening a little. It seemed to her she'd felt differently in her body back then. She'd lived in more of it. She was closer to the ground then.

She also remembered the particular kind of tiredness you got from being outside all day. It was a nice kind of tiredness, languid rather than grumpy. She had that feeling now.

The sun dipped behind the mountains and the valley glowed a beautiful color. Ama thought she recognized it from the poster.

She opted to sleep outside the tent that night. She wasn't sure why.

"I won't bring anybody in the tent. I swear," Carly pledged.

Ama laughed in spite of herself. "Thanks. But I just feel like being in the open tonight."

While she lay there, her ears tuned in to the many noises. There was the occasional snap of the fire dying yards away. There was the light wind blowing and rustling against every kind of thing. Most of all, there were the birds. There were many kinds of birds, and probably owls among them. There was a keening sound that could have come from a bird or a coyote or even a wolf. She expected her nerves to begin to coil, but they didn't. Her limbs felt heavy and loose, like they were sinking into the ground. She wasn't in a mood to be fearful, for some reason. She'd made it this far without being eaten by a wolf; she'd probably make it another night.

Who are you and what have you done with Ama? That was how Jo used to tease her when she acted in some way that was unexpected. It had been a long time since Ama had surprised herself.

She relaxed into the layers and layers of bird sounds. As she grew sleepy they stirred a memory even older than rolling down Pony Hill. The sounds stirred a deep-down feeling of Kumasi, where her memory existed in bits: images and sounds and smells rather than full scenes. The bird sounds were different there, but she did think of them. She thought of rough, squawky birds and delicate, whistling birds that stood and cried to her from the mango tree outside the front door. She thought of the birds that had settled in the courtyard where she used to play and how sometimes at a loud sound, like a blasting car horn, they'd all rise and fly away together. Ama pictured herself playing on a blanket on the grass and looking up and seeing the cloud of them against the bright sky.

She suddenly felt sad for her little brother, Bob, who'd been born here. She missed him achingly as she thought of him, with his baby teeth and his round head. He wouldn't have any of those things buried in his memory. He'd never had a mango tree outside his front door, only a carpeted hallway and two elevators.

Nicky and Katherine Rollins and Polly's body were playing pick-up sticks on the sunny carpet in the front hall of the Rollinses' overcooled house. Polly's mind had picked itself up and floated to its spot by the ceiling.

She was a better babysitter, she knew, when her mind stayed in her body, but she couldn't make it stay today.

Today she imagined herself not as the hungry, goosebumpy girl on the carpet below, but flattened into the pages of a magazine. She imagined her face in an ad for lip gloss or antiperspirant. But she imagined an altered version, a better, Photoshopped version of her face, with straighter teeth and knowing eyes.

She pictured piles and piles of the magazine with her face in it sitting in a warehouse. She imagined them getting tied up into blocks and trucked all over the country. She imagined them in the hold of a freight plane, going to other parts of the world. She imagined herself existing a little in every one of the magazines, bits of herself distributed to all the places the plane went.

She imagined appearing before the eyes of all the people who turned to her page—readers looking at her and her looking back at them. She imagined being seen and getting to see all the people she'd ever known and would someday know and even people she didn't know but wanted to know, like her father, for example. What if her father saw her there? Would he know her if he saw her? Would he think for a moment that he was looking at his own mother when she was young?

You could see so much more of the world when you were flat than when you were full. You could be in so many more places when you were weightless than when you were heavy. *I'd like to be two-dimensional,* she thought. That was what models got to be.

Seventeen

"Do you guys have plans for tonight?" Jo asked Megan as she brought an armful of menus back to the hostess station.

Megan looked tentative as she stacked the menus on the shelf. "Waitresses' night out," she explained apologetically. "Effie organized it."

"Well, my mom is away tonight. My house is totally empty. You guys should come over." Jo was surprised at how quickly and eagerly she played her trump card.

Megan looked sorry. "I don't know, Jo. I think Effie had something else in mind."

"We've got a lot of chips and stuff. My mom and I went to Costco over the weekend. We could invite the boys, too.

And I shouldn't really say this, but"—Jo dropped her voice—"the liquor cabinet is full."

The part of Jo's brain that wasn't talking was wondering why in the world she was saying the things she was saying. Her mom would find out if she had a bunch of people over and raided the liquor cabinet. She had never done anything like that before and she would get in huge trouble. Why was she offering it?

"Jo." Megan looked pained. "Maybe another time. Effie said no bussers. I didn't make the plans."

"I've hung out with you guys a ton of times this summer. Can't you tell Effie that?"

Megan made a face, and Jo wasn't sure she wanted to try to interpret it.

It had to do with Zach, she knew. Zach was in large part the secret of Jo's social success this summer, and now that Effie was back and claiming him, Jo had become controversial. No one seemed to want to look at her or talk to her today. She was to be avoided. And Zach was avoiding her too.

Why were they all willing to side with Effie right away? Jo was the one who had been around all summer. Did they all know that she and Zach had made out many times? That it was more than just a flirtation? She had as much of a claim on him as Effie did, if not more.

It was almost like everyone was scared of Effie, but Jo

wasn't going along with that. She was not scared of Effie. Let Effie be scared of her.

The last table cleared out by ten, seeming to know how little Jo wanted to get home. She watched the waitresses leave, all dressed up and made up. Overnight, Effie had become their ringleader, and apparently she was more hierarchical than the rest of them.

Jo couldn't go home to her empty house with nothing to do. She didn't want to call Bryn. She wished she could call Polly, but she'd been horrible to Polly. She was too guilt-ridden from not calling her dad to call her dad.

"I don't understand why you haven't called him," her mother had said to her before she left for Baltimore that morning.

"He can call me if he wants to talk," Jo had responded.

"Maybe he's concerned about having to talk to me in order to talk to you," her mother suggested. It was an honest and reasonable thing to consider.

"Maybe he could call my cell phone."

"Maybe dads don't understand about cell phones."

That was true in her dad's case. He carried a pager. He probably didn't even know her number.

Jo sat in the quiet back office for a while. She wondered what Ama was doing at that moment. Even after everything, she knew Ama would listen to her tale of woe and not sound happy about it. Ama was the kind of friend who was sad if you were sad. But she couldn't call Ama on her wilderness trip.

Jo decided on impulse to write a letter to Ama on the back of a paper children's menu. She didn't write about the restaurant or about Zach, but she did tell Ama about her parents. "They say it's a trial separation, but I have a feeling they are going to be pretty good at it. They've been practicing for a long time." At the end of the letter she wrote, "Enjoy the maze and word search." She stole an envelope from Jordan's desk—along with his two boxes of Tic Tacs—and addressed it to Ama's house, knowing Ama's mother would get it to her.

Hidalgo brought her some crab bisque with extra packets of the little round crackers.

"Thanks," she said to him, and tried to smile. *"Gracias."* She felt like she might cry and she wasn't even sure where it was coming from.

She wished she had called Polly the same afternoon she'd left. She wished she'd kept calling her until she'd reached her and apologized right away. She wished she had sent her a care package of chocolate chip cookies. She wished she could erase the words that she had said to Bryn that day. But Polly practically had a tape recorder in her ear. Though Polly might forgive her, there was no way she would forget.

At last Jo set out for home.

"Goldie."

Zach surprised her on the boardwalk.

Her heart surged at the sight of him. She couldn't help herself. "Hi," she said.

"What's up?"

I'm supposed to be mad at you, she told him in her mind. *You're a skank.* So why was she so happy? "I'm just heading home," she said.

He checked the time on his cell phone. "You've got twenty-five minutes until your curfew."

She was flattered that he still knew it. *It's only been a few days! Why wouldn't he know it?* she scolded herself.

"Can I walk you home on the beach?" he asked her.

"Don't you have a girlfriend?" she said. She meant it to sound pointed and mischievous, but it just sounded like a regular question.

He started walking anyway, and she went along behind him. "We're just walking," she added, quickening her step to catch his.

"You make it sound like I'm married or something," Zach said, grabbing her hand and swinging it. "Trust me, I'm not."

That shouldn't be good enough, said a voice in her head that sounded like Ama's.

You shouldn't trust him about anything. He doesn't deserve you, a voice like Polly's piped up.

But Jo didn't take her hand back. On the first night, Zach had told her she had strong hands. She still wanted to believe in him.

Believing in him shouldn't take this much effort, Ama told her.

Shut up, you guys! she said to Ama and Polly.

Instead of leading her down to the water, as he usually did, he led her up toward the lights of the boardwalk. She was surprised that he wanted to go back up onto the boardwalk, but it turned out he didn't. He led her underneath, to where it was dark and slightly drippy. Even the quality of the sand was different under here.

"Hey, Goldie?"

"Yeah."

"I think about you all day long."

When you aren't making out with Effie. That was what she should have said. But she didn't. She craved his attention so much it scared her a little. His eyes were on her and only her now, and she didn't want to challenge him or ruin it.

When he grabbed her free hand and held both of them, she let him. He was so dazzling to look at. He had a regular flush in his cheeks under his tan, giving his face more innocence than he deserved. He had a reckless and joyful expression that he wore nearly all the time. His posture was loose and his confidence was intoxicating.

She thought of ways to deflect his kiss, but she mostly hoped it would come. She would take what he offered. She couldn't help it. She wanted to be here and now and nowhere else. She didn't want to have to think.

He leaned in and kissed her. She made no effort to fend him off. He put his arms around her, his hands on her back, pushing her chest against his. She kissed him back. She stopped thinking altogether.

She felt his hands under her shirt, warm palms on her bare back. Her heart was pounding. *Don't make me think,* she told him in her mind. *Don't make me talk. I don't know how to say no right now.*

It wasn't Zach or his creeping hands that made her have to think. It was the sound of a shout and of powdery footsteps on the sand nearby.

She looked up, forced from her dream in jarring fashion. There was one girl nearby looking at them and three more farther away.

Zach let go of Jo and pulled away.

Jo recognized the face. It was Violet. She got close enough to let them see it was her and then scampered back to the group. Effie was there, Jo could see that clearly now. Megan and Sheba, too. All the girls were looking at Jo and Zach, now standing several feet apart.

Jo felt a cold, flat drip on the top of her head and it seemed to wake her up. God. What was she thinking? The two of them under the boardwalk. How tacky could you get?

Jo knew, instinctively and ominously, that for a girl like Effie, it was much worse discovering Jo and Zach at the same moment as her friends. There was no way for Effie to spin it or dodge it or gain some feeling of power over it. There was no way for her to save face, to make them all believe that Zach really did love her the best.

If Jo had doubted Zach when he said Effie wasn't his girlfriend before, she doubted him even more now. All the joy and the mischief were gone.

"I'm going to go," Jo said quietly to Zach. Under the gaze of many eyes, she pulled herself together and walked home.

She felt empty. She felt like she'd been scrounging crumbs off a dirty floor, wanting to believe she was getting a full meal. She felt like she hadn't truly eaten in many days.

She wished she could make her sadness go backward or even forward, to look back on it or postpone it, but it was here and now. How depressing of her to debase herself like that. How sad of her to try to find happiness in so little.

"Maman?"

"Ama?"

"Yes, it's me."

"What now? Are you all right?"

"Yes. I'm fine." Her voice was so much calmer this time. "Maureen let me call on the satellite phone."

"Where are you? You should be on your way to the air-port, I think. No?"

"We're still in Yosemite. Maman?"

"Yes?"

"I don't think I'm coming back tonight."

"Ama! *Pourquoi pas? Est-ce qu'il y a un problème?* They will drive you, won't they? The flight is confirmed."

"Yes. I know. They will drive me. But I think I should stay."

"Ama! Why?"

Ama was quiet for a minute. She was glad she was standing in a spot all by herself. "Because I think I should stay and finish."

"Ama, you don't owe them anything. You can do exactly what you want."

"I know. You're right. I guess . . . I want to."

"*You want to?* You said you hated it."

Ama sighed. "You're right. I know. I don't know how much I want to. There's one part of it—the rappel—that I'm dreading. But I feel like I should stay. Not because of them or you, because of me. Do you see what I mean? I think I'll be happier with myself if I stay." Ama thought of Polly's words, and how she had wanted them to be wrong.

"Are the group leaders telling you to stay?" her mother asked.

"No, Maman, they're not. I'm choosing."

"You're sure?"

"Yes." She looked down at her boots. "It's really beautiful here, you know."

"Is it?"

"It really is. It reminds me a little bit of Kumasi."

"Does it." That struck her mother silent for a moment.

After she'd said her good-byes and hung up the phone, Ama realized how much easier it was to stay now that she was allowed to go.

Jo got a text message from Bryn fifteen minutes before the lunch shift the next morning.

if i were u i wld call in sick

Jo had been planning to call in sick. She was still in her pajamas, in fact. She'd already made a few significant coughs in the kitchen in an attempt to convince herself and any neighbors who happened to see or hear her.

But now, staring at this message, she had to rethink it.

Everyone knew. Everyone. If anyone didn't know, Bryn would tell them. Probably even Hidalgo knew. Everyone was talking about it, and the shift hadn't even started yet.

What would Zach do?

She went to her room. She'd have to get dressed quickly. Maybe she was a hoochie girl and public enemy number one at the Surfside, but she wasn't a coward. She'd wear her scarlet A to work if she had to, but she would go. The fact that everybody already knew was strangely liberating.

Bryn was the first to see her when she walked through the door. She materialized by Jo's side in an instant.

"Did you get my message?" she asked urgently, under her breath.

Jo nodded.

"Then what are you doing here?" Bryn was barely breathing. This was the drama of the summer, and Bryn was clearly proud to play a role in it.

"What am I supposed to do? Call in sick for the rest of August?" Jo didn't bother to whisper in return.

"Violet says Effie is ready to kill. That's all I'm saying," Bryn hissed.

"If she kills me, there will be a lot of witnesses," Jo said. Part of being miserable was not caring as much what happened to you or who said what.

"Sorry, Jo, but you're crazy."

"Thanks for looking out for me," Jo said.

Jo put her stuff in her locker at the back of the restaurant and pulled her apron over her head. She saw Jordan as she passed by the office. She hoped he would put her on flatware, as he liked to do, but he seemed to sense that it would bring her relief today.

"You're on the floor today, Joseph," he barked at her. "Section one."

Jo hesitated for a moment. She cleared her throat. "Is Zach on?" she asked.

Jordan gave her a look. Even he knew. "He called in sick," he said.

Coward, Jo thought. She could hardly picture his face the way she had the day before. She wanted him to be somebody important, somebody whose love could change everything, but she couldn't make him be that today.

As she walked into the dining room she had a premonition that Jordan understood the workings of her misery more deeply than she had guessed. She suddenly knew who the lead waitress in section one would be without even needing to look. She wondered if he'd somehow found out about the Tic Tacs.

She saw Effie standing across the way in section one. Megan was there in section three. Violet was at the hostess station. Jo looked from one to the other. *How bad is it?* she wanted to ask Megan or Violet with her eyes, but neither of them looked back. Scott didn't look at her either, but he passed by humming "Under the Boardwalk."

Boy, you had to kiss another girl's boyfriend to know who your real friends were. In her case, that was no one.

It turned out there was one person who was willing

211

to look at her. One person, and unfortunately that person was Effie. The look was not pretty and it was not friendly.

Jo half considered going right up to Effie and apologizing. But what would she say, exactly? It hadn't been an accident or a mistake. Jo could sincerely pledge that she wouldn't do it again, but it was a bit late for that. She couldn't make Zach like Effie better, or make Effie care about him less. Zach's was the apology that could matter, and Jo couldn't give her that.

Anyway, the force field around Effie was so dark and scary, Jo couldn't get near enough to try.

"Bitch," Effie hissed at Jo as she strode by her to the kitchen.

Jo felt her cheeks reddening as she stood in place. She looked down at the vomit-brown carpet and up again. Still, no one dared look at her. She forcefully blinked back tears and went to the nearest waitress station to begin filling baskets with bread.

"I bet my tips are going to be terrible today," she said to Bryn as she went by, trying to sound light, but even Bryn had ceased speaking to her.

Jo didn't consider entering the staff room for lunch. She ate lunch in the kitchen with Carlos and Hidalgo. She was so grateful to them for talking with her, even if it was in Spanish. She used her halting Spanish to ask Hidalgo about his daughter. She brought them each two miniature candy bars after the rush resumed.

No one said another word to her until she was packing up to go home, absurdly grateful she was only working one shift today.

It was Effie, standing on the back step, towering over her.

"Don't come back," she warned.

"It's my job," Jo said bravely. She didn't step back or look away.

"Nobody wants you here."

"It's still my job," Jo said, and she turned and walked home.

In her quiet house, Jo sat in the kitchen, staring at nothing for a long time. She moved into her room and stared at nothing there for a longer stretch of time.

She looked at her trundle bed and thought of Polly. What she would give to have Polly there now.

She thought of her dad, alone in their other house. She pictured him surrounded by little white cartons of take-out Chinese food. He had been to China in his twenties, before he'd gotten married to her mom, and he always tried to order dishes in the restaurant by their proper Chinese names. She'd thought that was impressive when she was little and embarrassing when she was older.

She wished she had called him.

Eighteen

olly arrived home from her fifth babysitting job in five days, her heart trotting at the sight of the mail stacked on the hall table. She riffled through the pile, letting everything that wasn't from the IMTA glide to the floor.

It was here! Her nervous fingers were sloppy ripping the envelope open and unfolding the letter. A return card and envelope fell to the floor, but Polly was too agitated to pick them up.

It began:

> Dear Polly,
>   We are pleased to invite you to the twenty-third annual convention of the International Modeling and Talent Association.

That was it. She was in. She'd been accepted. She wasn't wrong to think she could do it. She'd been *invited*.

She scanned the rest of the page. It gave dates and directions and hotel information and payment instructions and blah blah. On the back of the page was a list in small print of all the modeling and talent agencies that would be represented. There were hundreds of them.

She had to go.

She ran to the phone in the kitchen and called Dia's studio number. When her mother didn't pick up, she called her cell phone. She got voice mail there as well. She hated leaving voice messages for Dia. Explaining herself seemed a guarantee that she wouldn't get a quick call back. Uncertainty and possible-emergency fears were her best chance. She called the studio number again. She hung up again on her mother's outgoing message.

Polly stared at the kitchen clock. She wished herself back in time to when she could call Jo or Ama anytime she liked—when they were happy to hear her voice. She wished she had somebody to tell.

She glanced out the front window. She probably would have told the neighbors or the garbageman if she could've. The mailman, of course, had already come and gone.

She even thought of calling Uncle Hoppy, at his old-age home, and he couldn't hear well enough to talk on the phone. He was a lip-reader. That idea seemed ridiculous to Polly when she pictured it.

She *really* needed to talk to Dia.

She stuck a ten-dollar bill and her house key in the front pocket of her jeans and strode out the door. Her mother's studio was at least three miles away, but Polly knew how to get there, and anyway, the walking would be good for calorie burning.

Dia had to say yes. She had to. Polly could pay for almost the whole thing if she kept babysitting at this rate. She'd earned $210 in the last five days alone. She'd put up flyers at the A&P for dog walking. She'd tell Mrs. Rollins and her other customers that she was available for even more babysitting. She'd go door-to-door in her neighborhood looking for work if it came to that.

Polly kept her mind busy calculating for most of the walk. First she calculated how many more hours she would need to work (eighty-five) to have enough to go to the convention ($1,160, including hotel and train tickets). When she'd figured that out she calculated the number of calories she'd eaten that day (340, so far) and the number of calories she could eat each day (1,100) in order to get to her new goal weight (102) by the day of the convention.

Entering the door of the building that housed her mother's studio, Polly suddenly stopped in uncertainty. The lobby surprised her, in part, by being small. Had it been so long since she'd last been here? She couldn't even think how long. The hallway, in all its flecked linoleum and sherbet-green plainness, was wrong-sized and shrouded in the murk of old memory.

The most recent picture she could dredge up of herself here was of her wearing the white beret she'd worn nearly every day in fourth grade. It couldn't really have been that long, could it?

Polly went on tentatively. She knew the right number of stairs to climb. That memory was in her legs. She knew the feel of the cold stairwell door's knob, though her height relative to it had changed. She felt its center lock, loose like a belly button against her palm.

The path to the studio door took fewer steps than it used to, but they were slower steps this time. She used to rush down this hall, its contours speeding her along the way the walls of a canyon sped a river.

She took her mother's doorknob in her hand, wondering whether to turn or knock. She knocked.

She realized she still had the letter, the invitation for the IMTA, clutched in her hand. She crushed it into her back pocket. She stood in a nervous hunch, picturing the studio on the other side. She pictured her mother coming to the door, not as she was now but as she used to look when Polly had come here a lot—before Dia had gotten her second and third tattoos and pierced her nose, when her hair was longer and she tied it back in a pink bandana when she worked. Polly remembered the loose purple bottoms Dia had called her harem pants, furry clogs, clay smudges drying into pale powder on her black turtleneck.

Polly knocked again. "Dia?" Her voice came up as a croak through layers and hours of quiet. She cleared her throat. "Hey, Dia? Are you in there?"

Did she hear something? A rustle? A whir?

She knocked a third time, and when she heard no answer, she tried the knob. It turned, though she wasn't expecting it to. She pushed the door cautiously open. Sunshine poured in the tall windows, whiting out her vision for a few seconds. She took small steps in.

"Dia? Hello?"

She looked around, worried for a moment that she hadn't remembered the way after all.

This couldn't be her mother's studio, because that was so full, and this place was empty. Polly scanned the walls for the familiar piles, but they weren't there. She saw two armatures by the back corner on the left, caked with old clay but unused.

Her mother's studio was packed with sculptures and supplies and papered with sketches. Where were they? Where were the huge bins of old broken cell phones, batteries, wristwatches, and computer parts? Dia spent almost every day of Polly's life in the studio. Why weren't her things here?

Slowly Polly turned to look to the right. She pushed her eyes along the wall until they reached the little desk, her old desk, where she'd drawn pictures while her mother worked. That was still there, though it had only a laptop on it now. Pushing farther, she saw the old cot in the right back corner, where she used to sleep. And feeling like the baby bear in Goldilocks, she recognized with a dawning strangeness that her bed had someone in it.

"Dia?" Polly's voice was small and her mother didn't stir.

Her mother was asleep in the little cot, curled at the middle, bare feet hanging past the foot of it, her face turned away, toward the back wall.

Besides the desk and the cot there was a TV sitting on an old nightstand a few feet past the foot of the bed. And besides those things, Polly saw that there were bottles lined up two deep along the back wall. They were mostly wine bottles, uncorked and empty.

Polly suddenly felt scared to be there. She wanted her mother to comfort her and explain what was going on, but it was also Dia she was scared of. It wasn't quite her mother in this changed place with her back to her, but Polly felt that if she turned and Polly could see her face, Dia would be her mother again.

"Dia?" Polly heard the tears in the back of her voice. She ventured closer on soft feet. *Come back. Don't be mad at me.*

Her steps took her close enough to see into what had once been the storage closet. Polly remembered many years ago when her mother had removed the hinges with a screwdriver, wrested the closet door from its place, and carried it down to the street, with Polly helping and cheering her along. The floor space had become a little alcove where her mother had showcased pieces of her work. Polly had been amazed that you could just do that—just join a closet to a room with your own hands. Her mother could.

Now there were piles of books covering the little rectangle of wood floor, and above them, hanging in a vertical row of three, were drawings on paper, her mother's only work on display. They showed three different views of her, Polly, sleeping. They were from a long time ago, the way she used to be.

Jo sat at the computer for a long time that afternoon composing an e-mail. It was handy, in a way, that there was no one in her house after her lunch shift. It gave her the freedom to cry as much as she felt like without anyone seeing or hearing her. Also it gave her time to try all the possible versions of her letter. She tried the nice version, the practical version, and the well-written version and finally settled on the honest version.

To: PollyWog444
From: Jobodobo
Subject: shame and woe

Dear Polly,

I am sorry for what happened when you
visited. I know you must have overheard the
things I said to Bryn, and I feel miserable
every time I think of it—which I do a lot.

The truth is I really didn't want you to visit.
I know that's mean and I'm ashamed of it.
I was so caught up with the scene at the
restaurant and these older girls and this
guy I was kind of hooking up with. I just
thought that was the most important thing
and that you would get in the way of it.
Even though it's not really fair to you,
that's what I thought.

It's kind of scary to be so wrong. In fact,
it's really scary. But I was. Those people
weren't important. They weren't real
friends at all. But you are. I understand
that better now. No matter what happens, I
will always know what a real friend is
because of you and Ama.

I don't expect you to forgive me. I don't
really think you should. But I just want to
tell you the truth, because what I said to
Bryn was a lie. You are my friend. Even if
we never talk to each other again, you
have been a better friend than I have ever
deserved.

Love,
Jo

Because of the stance of the weeping willow, the tree has long been associated with grief.

Nineteen

"I don't think he's coming back," Richard, the manager, said about Zach.

"What do you mean?" Jo asked.

"He hasn't shown up for three shifts in a row. That means we've seen the last of him. Anyway, if he did come back I'd probably have to fire him." Richard punched a few buttons on his phone. "It happens in August. Waiters at a beach-town restaurant aren't the most dependable people in the world."

Jo nodded. "They aren't, are they?"

Jordan must have done the schedule again. Jo found herself back in Effie's section. What a bitter sense of humor he had.

Jo withstood the glares and hisses. She was getting used to the averted eyes and the whispers. Even Bryn was trashing her to the older girls, delighted at last to have something to offer them.

By nine o'clock Jo's feet were aching and she suddenly worried she was going to cry.

She walked out front, where none of the waitstaff took their breaks. She went all the way across the sand and down to the surf, flung off her shoes, and wet her feet. The enormity of the ocean made her feel meaningless, but today that was a comfort. Zach was meaningless and Effie was meaningless and this stupid summer was meaningless too.

When she walked back up she saw a young woman waiting on the bench by the restaurant's front entrance.

"Hi," Jo said for no particular reason, other than that the young woman had a striking and sympathetic face.

"Hi," the young woman said back.

"Are you waiting for someone?" Jo asked. She was starved for company, she knew. Strangers were friendlier than so-called friends.

"One of the waitresses. Do you know Effie Kaligaris?" she asked.

Jo took that as her cue to get back to work. She ran into Bryn by the lockers. "There's a girl out front waiting for Effie," she told Bryn, even though Bryn wasn't speaking to her. "I think she's the most beautiful girl I've ever seen."

Bryn couldn't resist knowing something. "That's Effie's sister. Her name is Lena. She just came back from Europe."

"Her name is Lena? Are you sure? Are you sure she's Effie's sister?"

"Yeah."

"You're kidding."

Bryn rolled her eyes. "And I would be kidding because why?"

"I think she's one of the Sisterhood. You know, with the pants. I think she's one of those girls." Jo was almost breathless. She felt like she'd seen a movie star. She suddenly wanted to call Ama and Polly and tell them. She wished she could.

Bryn narrowed her eyes. "Simmer down, sister," she said mockingly.

Jo stood on her tiptoes to catch another glimpse of Lena, but she had gone.

"No wonder Effie's so sour," Jo murmured.

"What's that supposed to mean?"

"How would you like to have a sister like that?"

For the last hour of the shift, Effie was more pleasant. Or less radically unpleasant. Maybe she was cowed by the presence of her sister, Jo conjectured. Maybe she was realizing what a complete wretch she was being. Maybe the worst of it was over.

That was what Jo thought until she was carrying a tray of drinks on one hand and a wipe rag in the other toward table four. Her feet were hurting worse than ever and her hand was shaking under the weight of the heavy tray.

She maneuvered herself to the right spot at the side of the table and began lowering the tray. She silently cursed herself for carrying the rag, because she couldn't put it down anywhere and she needed the second hand for balance. She bent her knees and leaned over the four-top, between a pregnant woman and a man, presumably her husband.

This was when Effie passed by, more shadow than person. Effie took corporeal shape only long enough to sense the moment of Jo's greatest instability and knock her in the hip. Jo felt herself going down, and there was nothing she could do. Time spread out so she could see and suffer every aspect of the catastrophe.

It wouldn't have been so bad if the drinks she'd flung at the table were seltzers, say, or ginger ales, rather than three very full glasses of red wine and one cranberry spritzer.

It wouldn't have been so bad if they had just crashed to the floor rather than shattering and bouncing on the table in such a way as to produce a literal cascade of red liquid and glass shards.

It wouldn't have been so bad if the shoulder of the man

she had grabbed for balance was healthy and normal rather than in a sling because of having been recently dislocated.

After the droplets and bits of glass had finally been carried down by gravity, the five of them—Jo and her four customers—along with all the other people in the restaurant, froze in blinking disbelief, making sure no glass had landed in their eyes or mouth.

Jo found her voice, eventually, and soon after that her hands. She began apologizing and brushing the glass from arms and shoulders.

The man with the bad shoulder groaned and clasped it with his good arm. The other three stood all at once, sending lapfuls of glass bits to the floor.

While the rest of the staff stood dumb and motionless, Carlos appeared with a roll of paper towels under one arm and the broom and dustpan in the other.

"Thank you, Carlos," Jo whispered in a voice just this side of a sob.

He patted her arm. More glass fell to the floor. She wondered if she was allowed to cry yet.

Richard, the manager, marched out, closely followed by Jordan. Jordan was shaking his head.

There were a lot of apologies. Jo heard herself making most of them. There were guarantees of dinner on the house and all that. The four diners were in a pretty big hurry to get out of that place. They could have yelled at Jo even more than they did but for their hurry.

She heard Richard ominously assure the departing diners that he would "take care of her." What did that mean? Was he going to order her out back and shoot her?

She watched the four diners file out under the care of the fast-talking Richard, all of them more or less covered with dark red liquid.

God, it looked grim. It looked like a scene from a horror movie—at the end, not the beginning. It wouldn't have been so bad if the pregnant woman hadn't been wearing a white dress.

"Polly?" Dia sat up, disoriented. "Polly! What are you doing here? Is everything okay?"

Polly felt numb and jointless. She didn't know whether to go forward to her mother or step back. "Everything is okay."

"How did you get here?"

"I walked."

The alarm retreated from Dia's face and her reorientation began. She looked around the studio and back at Polly. "What are you doing here?" she asked again, in a different tone.

"I—I . . ." Polly touched the balled-up paper in her back pocket. "Nothing. No reason."

"You walked all the way here for no reason?"

"My . . . I thought . . ." Polly couldn't think of why she'd come. She couldn't think of the name of the convention she'd wanted to go to. "I'll leave," she said.

"Polly." Her mother wrapped her arms around herself, as though it was cold, even though it was hot.

Her mother had missed countless lunches and dinners. She had missed drop-offs and pickups from school. She'd missed the soccer games where Polly mostly sat on the bench and twisted grass in her fingertips until they turned green. She'd missed Polly's plays and playdates. She'd left off scheduling things like dentist's appointments and piano lessons, because she had to, *had to* get to the studio. Polly had imagined there would be sculptures, hundreds of sculptures, for all the things she'd missed. Where were they? What did it mean? What did her mother do when she came here?

Polly didn't want to look at her mother or have her explain anything. "See you at home," she murmured.

"Polly, wait. What's in your back pocket?" Dia asked. She unwrapped herself and stood.

Polly touched her hand to it again. "It's nothing."

"Let me see."

Polly dutifully took it from her pocket. Her mother walked closer, and she handed it to her. Dia flattened it out to read it.

"It's from the modeling thing in New York. You got in."

"Yes."

"You must be happy."

Polly didn't know what she felt right then, but she didn't think it was happy.

"And you want to go, I bet."

Polly shrugged. She felt tired. She wanted to go to sleep. "If you can't take me, that's okay."

Dia's eyes darted from one part of the empty room to another part as she considered. "Maybe I could take you. Maybe it would be good for me to get up to New York for a few days."

Polly didn't move her head or say anything.

"You know, I think it could be good. Let's go home and look at the dates and the train schedules and how much it'll cost and see if we can figure it out."

Polly followed Dia out of the studio and watched her lock the door. She thought of the questions she wasn't asking and the answers Dia wasn't giving. She wondered what kind of bargain she and her mother were deciding to make.

Jo cleaned wine, juice, and bits of glass until she was summoned to the office. She trudged through the dining area feeling that the space was endless and all eyes were upon her.

"Hi," Jo said wearily, standing in front of Richard's desk. It seemed, somehow, like the wrong thing to say.

"Jo."

"Yeah."

"I'm afraid this is a fire-able offense. And an expensive one too."

She nodded.

"I know it was an accident. But my God, what an accident."

She nodded again. It was an accident on her part, not on Effie's. She could have said that, but she didn't feel like it. She didn't want to entangle herself with Effie any more than she already had.

"You've been a really fine bus girl up until this point."

"Thanks," she mumbled.

Jordan hovered around the doorway. Jo felt like punching him.

"I'll quit if that makes it any easier," she offered.

Richard sighed. "Either way."

"Okay, well. Thanks. And sorry about everything."

"You take care, Jo."

Jordan jumped out of the way to let her pass. She left her apron in the kitchen. Hidalgo gave her a hug and Carlos patted her arm. She hurried out the door so nobody would see her cry.

She didn't realize until she was out the door and felt the

cool breeze on her skin that she too was covered in sticky red liquid.

Jo couldn't go home. She wandered around on the beach for a while, trying to figure out what to do. She had been so excited about the nights when her house would be empty. She had pictured parties, making out, mocking her curfew. She had imagined the freedom. Now freedom was emptiness and the emptiness was intolerable.

She had an idea. Instead of walking home, she turned and walked back toward town. She had money in her pocket and no place to be. She had no one waiting for her anywhere, no one she could see who wanted to see her. She had no job to go to tomorrow.

She looked up at the sky and imagined Ama looking at the sky on some mountain someplace, and Polly looking at the sky from the window by her bed.

She pictured Zach, and the picture made her stomach bunch. She had propped him up with her hopes and her needs, and without them he fell straight through the floor.

Freedom shmeedom. She had more of it than she needed. *It's not as great as you think it's going to be,* she felt like telling her dad.

The bus was once again close to empty. This time her near neighbor was an older woman with elastic-waist pants and penciled-in eyebrows. She was not as cute as

Zach, certainly, and she would get Jo into a lot less trouble.

"Do you need to see a doctor?" the lady asked, straining to see Jo, her face full of concern.

Jo touched her stiff hair and then moved her fingertips to a patch of wine that was still drying on her T-shirt. "Oh, it's not blood," she explained. "It's wine." By the look on the woman's face, that wasn't much of a comfort.

Jo smelled the sweet, sickly fragrance of it, topped off by the smell of the cranberry juice.

On the bus ride, she fell asleep for a time and dreamed about the beautiful girl, Effie's sister, covered in wine. She dreamed of Finn sledding with her down Pony Hill, but she was older and he was still young. She dreamed of getting lost in her own house.

Luckily she had enough cash left to take a cab from the bus station to her house. She feared that if she walked, her fellow pedestrians might feel the need to call the police or an ambulance at the sight of her.

She rang the doorbell of her house as though she was a stranger there. Was her dad working late? Was he sleeping over at some woman's house? Would she catch him on a date? Was that why he was in such a hurry to get unmarried?

The door opened and there he was. He didn't look like he was on a date. He was wearing shorts and an undershirt and slippers and his bifocals on a chain around his neck. His hair was rumpled.

"Jo," he said, his expression evolving into alarm as he saw the red stains on her face and shirt. "What happened to you?" He grabbed hold of her like she was four and not fourteen.

"It's okay," she protested from the folds of his shirt. "It's just wine."

He let her go to look at her. "Why have you got wine all over you?"

"I spilled it."

"Were you drinking? Did you get locked out at the beach? Where is your mom?"

Though long out of practice, he was full of parental worry.

"No. I spilled it at my job. At the restaurant. And I got fired, so I came home."

He nodded. He did her the kindness of acting like all of that sounded reasonable.

"Come inside. Do you want to take a shower? Have you eaten?" It was funny how he had suddenly turned into her mother hen.

"Yes. No, I haven't eaten."

"I'll make you something. Go take a shower and get dressed, and then you can tell me what happened."

• • •

235

All the way along the death march to the dreaded cliff of no return, Noah walked beside her. Ama mostly kept to herself, while Noah kept trying to start a conversation.

"How are your feet?"

"Better," she said.

"Blisters?"

"Healed."

"Wow. That's great."

They walked on in silence.

"Do you want some gorp? I have an extra bag."

Gorp was like gold by that point. Nobody had any left. She thought of the M&M's. Her mouth began to water, but she stayed strong. "No thanks."

They crossed a little river. Ama was surprised at how easily she stepped from stone to stone without slipping or losing her balance under her forty-pound pack. They walked up a hill and down it.

"Do you know about Model UN?" he asked after a while.

Ama nodded. Her sister had done Model UN. Ama wanted to do it too, but she didn't feel like telling him so. "How come?"

"You should do it next year."

"You think?"

"Yeah. It's cool. We could hang out."

She looked down and she didn't say anything.

"It's not until the spring, though." He laughed self-consciously. "So I guess maybe it would be easier if I just asked for your number."

Ama couldn't take it anymore. She stopped walking and he stopped too. "Hey, Noah?"

"Yeah."

"Can I ask you something?"

"Okay."

"If you want my number, then why were you making out with Carly?" She couldn't hold it in.

Noah stared at her. Confusion turned to indignation. He looked as though she'd accused him of boiling rabbits. "What are you talking about? I didn't make out with Carly."

He was quite the actor, wasn't he? "Yes, you did. At least twice. Once in my own tent. That was hard to miss."

Noah looked angry now. "No, I didn't, Ama. Not even once. Not in your tent and not anywhere else. No offense, but you don't know what you're talking about."

His certainty made Ama step back and wonder. Had she really, really seen his face? Was she really, really sure it was him? She tried to picture his face in her tent on that fateful night before she'd huffed out of the tent and slept on the anthill. She couldn't. She could picture a back and hair she thought was his, but not his face. Could she have been wrong all this time? But she was so certain of it. "Are you sure?" she said timidly.

"I think I would know."

She chewed the inside of her cheek. "Carly made out with everybody else," she pointed out.

"Yeah, well. Not me."

He still looked upset, and she felt a little bit guilty, but she also felt a lightness like bubbles in her stomach.

"Maybe you forgot," she said mischievously.

"Shut up." He pretended to punch her arm.

She punched his back, not so pretend.

"Ow." He tried to punch hers again, but she dodged him. She laughed.

They walked along. Up another hill and down. She felt the soft pine needles under her boots. She looked up happily at the sky. She slapped his hand in a friendly way. "Can I have that gorp?" she asked.

Twenty

Jo heard her father in the kitchen before she saw him there. He was crashing around, opening things and dropping things.

The feel of the house was different, she thought as she walked past the living room. It was a little dustier, maybe, and more cluttered, with fewer lights on. The pillows didn't look as pert and the violets in the window were barely hanging in.

The windows were open. That was the main thing, she realized. It was not uncomfortably hot in the house—in fact, it was a nice cool night. But the steaminess of summer, the deep August scent of ripeness, had crept into the rooms, where it was usually shut out.

That was the big difference. Her mother was very big on climate control. The inside and outside air did not usually mix.

The house wasn't abandoned, as she had half expected. It was the opposite. It looked surprisingly, unusually lived-in. Her dad's newspapers and medical journals sprawled over the dining room table. His slippers were discarded in the living room; his book was left open on the couch. Coffee mugs and glasses sat on various surfaces — and not a coaster in sight. What would her mother say?

In the kitchen, a flame burned under a pan, but the pan was empty, as far as she could tell. She hoped her dad wouldn't burn the house down. Almost every drawer and cabinet in the place stood open. It felt so different from the way her mother occupied this room.

"What are you making?" she asked.

"Tacos," he answered brightly.

"Wow."

"I know. I've been doing some cooking this summer."

He stood up from the under-counter cabinet in which he had been foraging. He looked so proud it almost broke her heart.

When he poured some olive oil into the empty pan it sizzled wildly and smoked. Her father jumped back. "Will you look at that," he said.

She tried not to wince. "Do you need help?"

He adjusted the heat under the pan. "You can grate the cheese," he offered.

"Okay," she said.

She dutifully grated as he opened more things and dropped more things and landed some other things in his pan.

"You probably don't think I know my way around the kitchen," he said, concentrating on reading the spice jars, "but do you remember I used to make dinner for you and Finn every Tuesday and Thursday night when your mother worked?"

"You did?" It felt like such a strange and unexpected liberation that her dad said Finn's name like that, just throwing it into the mix along with the chili pepper and the chopped lettuce. They couldn't do that around her mother. Her mother became stricken and left the room, so they'd learned not to do it, but Jo yearned to. She yearned to talk about Finn, not in a hallowed or sad way, but just remembering that he had been there too, in the regular ways.

"Yes. I didn't make big things like tacos," her father remembered. "But I made chicken and rice. I made a meat loaf once."

"Did you really?"

"You don't remember?"

She wanted to remember. "I think I do. A little."

"You loved peas. I always made peas."

"Finn loved peas," Jo said.

Her father nodded. "He really did."

"I still love them."

"Do you?"

"Yes."

He nearly bounded over to the freezer. He got out a brick of them and showed her.

She laughed. She couldn't remember the last time she'd laughed.

"I'm finished with the cheese. Can I do anything else?" she asked.

She was worried about his tacos, based on the strange brew forming in his pan and the pure chaos on the counters. She realized she didn't want him to fail. She wanted them to be good.

He set her up with a cutting board and a paring knife and an avocado. She was oddly pleased that he trusted her with a good sharp knife.

"It's nice to cook with company," he said to her after an amicable silence.

She nodded. She sensed he'd been alone as much as she had. She sensed he had enjoyed his freedom this summer about as well as she had enjoyed hers.

Usually Jo liked to keep the various items on her plate separate, but in the case of her dad's taco dinner, that wasn't going to be possible. Like it or not, the salsa mixed with the sour cream and flooded the tortilla, which edged into the puddle of beans and shared a messy border with the guacamole, and all of it sat under a thatch of melting cheese.

Her dad raised his bottle of beer to her glass of milk. She'd almost laughed when she'd seen him pouring her milk, like she was still six. She'd almost rejected it, but now as she drank it, she couldn't imagine anything tasting better.

"Cheers," he said.

"Cheers," she said back. She didn't know what else to say.

"Well, dig in," he said.

She took a deep breath and dug in, letting the multitude of textures and temperatures heap on her fork. She took a tentative bite and then a more confident one. She took another one, with extra salsa. The smell of it all wrapped around her head and the taste blotted out most of her other senses. She was so hungry.

She ate and ate. She poured on more salsa and sprinkled more cheese. She found she could barely look up from her food or stop eating long enough to talk. But finally, she made herself pause. She looked up at her dad and said to him, "These are really, really good." And they were.

Her stomach got fuller and fuller, but she kept eating. "Is there more?" she asked.

Her father looked pleased. "Yes. Plenty. Plenty more in the kitchen."

He served her a second plate and watched her eat. With his glasses off, she saw his eyes.

"Jo?"

"Yeah?"

"I'm happy you came home."

At first, Polly had exaggerated to herself a little how much weight she'd lost. She was excited and proud of herself so she rounded up. If the scale said she'd lost 4.6 pounds, she called it 5.

But now that she'd lost more than she'd planned, she'd started to exaggerate the other way. She'd lost 13.8 pounds, but she told herself it was 12, figuring she'd weighed herself a little wrong when she started.

Now, instead of weighing herself first thing in the morning after she'd peed, she'd begun weighing herself later in the day, after she'd eaten something and had a big glass of water. She didn't want to have to stop yet.

I am small, she thought, losing herself in the volume of her red cotton pants as she dressed in the bathroom. She was used to growing out of clothes, but now she was going the other way, almost like she was turning back the clock. It was consoling to think you could do that. The past was a lot easier to imagine than the future. She pictured herself going to a clothing store and getting a *smaller* size. Even her bras had finally gotten too big. Yesterday she'd gone into the back of her drawer and fished out the first bra she'd gotten, in sixth grade.

Maybe I really could be a model, she thought, shivering a little in the sunshine coming through the bathroom window. The skin of her arms looked mottled sticking out of her T-shirt. The dark hair on her arms seemed more plentiful and longer than before. Her favorite silver bracelet, the one Dia had bought for her at an antiques shop in Philadelphia, sagged on her thin wrist.

She did her arm-swinging, calorie-burning walk back to her bedroom. *Burning.* That was a strange word for it, wasn't it?

She had to get ready in a hurry because she had the Rollins kids at ten-thirty and then a toddler named Ryan at four. Ryan's mom was a new customer, referred to her by Mrs. Rollins, and she wanted to make a good impression.

Dia said Polly didn't have to earn any more money, that she would cover the rest, but Polly liked working and having places to go all day.

Polly bought the train tickets to New York online, one for her, one for Dia. Dia didn't want to hang around the modeling convention, but she said they could have a nice time together in New York and go to the Metropolitan Museum. Dia planned to meet with the people from her art gallery at the same time as the big runway show, but Polly didn't really mind.

The trip wasn't for a few more days, but Polly had already started packing. She left her suitcase open on the floor. At various times of the day she'd put things in and take them out and put different things in. She put in her research report on models and then she took it out again. She didn't know if she'd find anyone at the IMTA who would be interested in it. She felt a little silly looking at the cover she'd drawn for it, though she'd felt proud of it at the time.

She missed Ama and Jo. She couldn't help it. She had gone a long time without them. So long that she feared she was losing the knack of having friends or being one. Ama and Jo always knew her best and helped her know herself. They knew the shape of who she was, and helped keep her in it. Without them she felt like she drifted and lost her outlines.

It was painful to think of ninth grade without being close to them, but she had forced herself to do it. The e-mail from Jo had given her hope, but she was afraid to hope very much. It was probably good for her to practice being alone.

Jo couldn't fall asleep that night. She walked downstairs, enjoying the shafts of moonlight sliding in through the glass on either side of the big front door. In her T-shirt and boxer shorts she floated into the living room and sat on the couch. It was nicer in here with her dad's stuff all around it. She hated coasters. It was nicer in here with the heady, green summer air.

It gave her an aching nostalgia, the smell of summer in this room. In the old days, when Finn was still alive, her mom had left the windows open. Jo could remember the feeling of it.

It made her wonder about this house, how her mom had kept it so perfect, with Mona, the housekeeper, under strict orders to clean up your stuff practically before you'd even left it anywhere. Her mom lavished money and attention on the house, just the way she lavished it on her body and her face and her hair, her "upkeep," as she called it. Jo had always believed that her mom wanted to make everything perfect for her family. But now she wondered. What was it really for?

It was strange to see her dad's stuff. She wasn't used to seeing the books and papers he was reading, the crossword half done, and a Sudoku puzzle with a penciled number in every square. Who knew her dad liked Sudoku?

It was strange to think of her dad teaching himself how to cook this summer, alone in the kitchen, when he hardly even came home for dinner.

She'd thought that when he was free of her mom, he would stay at the office or the hospital day and night and leave only to go to parties with cute female residents or nurses. But there was no evidence of that. Just the opposite. When he was free of her mom, he came home.

Jo began to get a feeling, faraway but powerful, of just how unhappy they had been, how much had been sacrificed because of it.

After Finn had died, her dad had gone to work. Jo knew that. He'd pushed himself harder and harder. She'd sensed, even when she was younger, that he was driven by the desire for distraction and forgetting. "You try to feel in control of something," he'd said to the therapist in one of the few family grief sessions her mother had been able to tolerate.

Jo thought of her mother's immaculate house and immaculate appearance and her endless badgering about where you put your glass down. Jo now wondered if her mother was trying to control some things too. It hadn't always been like that.

Jo's stomach grumbled and she realized she was hungry again. She walked into the kitchen and piled leftovers of everything into a jumble on her plate. When she went into the freezer to get ice for her water, she saw the three boxes of peas, covered in white frost.

Her dad might never be able to talk to her honestly about what had happened with her mother. He would probably always be a little awkward with her and afraid to ask her questions. Maybe he would never know her cell phone number.

But there were peas where there hadn't been peas in a long time. Love didn't necessarily look the way you expected it to.

Twenty-one

Early in the morning Ama sat at the edge of the world, wondering why she was so willing to fall off it.

"Jonathan goes and then it's your turn," Maureen called to her.

"But I thought I got to go last," Ama said squeakily.

"You are last," Maureen said affectionately. Maureen hadn't said much about it, but Ama knew how relieved and happy she was that Ama had chosen to stay.

Ama watched in bewilderment as Jonathan practically leapt off the cliff when his turn came. He didn't even check his ropes. He didn't even make the proper signal to his be-layer. He looked like he would have jumped off as eagerly with or without ropes.

"He's crazy," Ama commented.

"He is. And stupid," Jared said.

Ama considered that. "So if I'm petrified, does that mean I'm smart?"

"Absolutely," Jared said. He looked over the edge, watching Jonathan make his swift descent. "All right, he's down." Jared shook his head. "Crikey. I don't think he could have done it any faster if he'd fallen."

Ama hoisted herself doubtfully to her feet. "I guess that means it's my turn." She was so trussed up with ropes and gear she could barely move.

"Yes, it does."

"Am I really going to do this?"

"Yes!" he and Maureen both answered.

Ama teetered closer to the edge. She couldn't even look. If she couldn't look over it, how could she go over it?

Maureen was her belayer. Jared helped Ama clip herself in. Ama checked her ropes and her connections about fifteen times.

"I think you're good," Jared said. He smiled at her.

"You think?" she asked earnestly.

"Yep."

"Go get 'em, honey," Maureen said.

Ama crept closer to the abyss. Her hands were soaked with sweat.

Two more feet and her eyes met with a view that

astonished her *Oh, my.* Down below was a cobalt river snaking through a green valley with fields of flowers. Beyond she could see pine trees etched against towering blue mountains. It really was just like in the poster.

She drew in a deep breath, one of her first of the summer. She looked out across the lovely landscape and up at the cloudless, seamless sky. She had become well acquainted with roots and dirt and bugs this summer, she realized. Before that she had spent a lot of time in the classroom and the library and in her bedroom at her desk. But she hadn't spent much time looking at the sky.

She remembered the old days when she and Jo and Polly would lie on the grass in Jo's backyard on summer nights and look at the stars. The world had seemed much bigger then, like it contained more possibilities, more ways to be.

"You ready?" Jared asked.

"I think so," she breathed.

How were you supposed to get over the edge? Everyone else had made it look so effortless she hadn't even noticed how they'd done it. She got down on all fours and backed up, like a horse backing into her stall. Her helmet fell over her eyes. She felt like her one talent in life was for making things effortful.

"On belay!" Maureen called, starting Ama on her official descent.

"Climbing," Ama responded in a strangled voice.

She put one knee over the edge. Her foot found nothing but air. She looked over her shoulder. *Oh, my God.* She saw all the tiny figures of her group looking up at her. She thought she saw the miniature plane of Noah's hand, turned up in a wave. It didn't look like 350 feet down. It looked like at least a thousand. Who had done the measuring here? *This is nothing like Pony Hill,* she felt like saying to Polly.

Her foot dangled against nothing. She shifted her second knee over the edge. Both feet dangled against nothing. She was stuck in her awkward position.

Jared bent down and adjusted her helmet. He took both of her hands in his. He must have noticed they were soaking. He gave her another encouraging smile. "You know, Ama, you're a lot more courageous than Jonathan," he said.

Ama squinted one eye against the sun. "Are you joking?"

"Courage is the conquest of fear, right? He had no fear. You have a lot."

"I have a lot," she echoed. She wasn't going to pretend otherwise. Who was she kidding?

He lifted her by her two hands as she wriggled back over the edge. At last her feet found purchase against the rock.

"Okay. You've got to lean back," Jared instructed her.

"No . . . I don't. . . . Really?"

"Yes, you do."

She squeezed her eyes shut and leaned a few inches. "Like this."

"Yes!"

"Don't let go!" she screamed at him. The wind was blowing harder out here over the edge. She felt herself swinging slightly. "Ahhhhhhh!"

"It's okay. I won't let go. I've got you."

Ama looked back over her shoulder again. Her heart was thumping so powerfully she was amazed it hadn't launched itself right out of her body and into the sky.

"Keep going," Jared told her.

"I'm going," she said. She moved about another millimeter.

"Trust the rope, Ama."

She felt another gust of wind. She clutched Jared's hands for all she was worth.

She looked up at him and noticed he was wincing in pain. "I think I may have to get all my fingers amputated after this," he said, but he managed to smile through it.

"Sorry," she murmured. She remembered his handshake on the first day at the airport. She tried to loosen her death grip a little.

Ama glanced over her shoulder again. She looked at the rock in front of her. For some reason she thought of the first day of third grade, the day she'd met Jo and Polly and they'd escaped from school together. She remembered so vividly looking at the doors of school, wanting to go back in, but wanting to go with them even more. *You can do it,* Jo had said to her. And she had. It had been her greatest thrill, the start of her life's best adventure.

Ama looked back over her shoulder at the tiny people standing on hard ground below. *You can do it,* she said to herself, missing Jo and Polly and herself, the way she used to be. *And if not, then you'll die and so who cares.*

Ama took one more big breath before she let go. She half expected it to be her last. She half expected to hurtle down to the ground in a heap. But she didn't.

"Open your eyes," Jared told her.

Oh. She'd forgotten about that. She opened them and saw that the rope held her fast. She was slightly surprised that Jared was still there. She imagined he might be small and far above her, but there he was, big as before, massaging his fingers.

She took a step backward down the cliff. A tiny, quivering one. She took another.

"Lean back. Trust the rope," he told her.

She looked so hard at the rope in front of her, her eyes crossed. Could she trust it? She imagined Maureen on the other end. She was happy that it was Maureen.

She took more steps. Jared was getting smaller.

A hard gust shook her. She grabbed the rope with both hands and tried to take charge of her weight by pulling her body vertical.

She immediately lost her footing, screamed, scratched madly at the rock face, and nearly went into cardiac arrest.

"Falling!" she cried to her belayer.

But then the wind calmed and when she made herself stop flailing she discovered that she was just hanging there, just dangling by the rope like a spider at the end of her thread.

I can't really mess this up, she thought with dawning jubilation.

Once again she planted her feet against the rock and began to lean back. She understood now that you couldn't keep your footing if you weren't willing to lean out and give up your weight. It was like many other things in camping and hiking: the worse and more terrifying and more counterintuitive it was, the more it was the thing you were supposed to do.

She leaned back even farther, so that her back was nearly parallel with the ground, assuming the ground was somewhere down there. The steps were easier this way. Her feet really stuck to the rock.

She bent her knees and made a tiny, brave jump from the rock. She heard cheering from below, and from Jared and even Maureen above. She smiled to herself.

She took a moment to look around her, at the quiet valley, at the streams of condensation in the sky, at the curling roots of the trees determinedly making a home in the cliff.

Behind her the world laid itself out in a patchwork so vast she felt like she could see all the way to Bethesda and to Pony Hill. She imagined that if she tried she could see all the way across the ocean to the little house in Kumasi and her mango tree. Polly was more right than she even knew. This was a view not to be missed.

Ama picked up her pace. She walked and even pushed off and bounced now and then. The next time she looked around her she realized that Jared was now smaller than Dan and Noah and Carly and the rest of the group below her. *Unbelievable.*

Jared waved. He knew she had it now.

I'm in the air, she thought. She waved her arms around a little to feel it was just air. She really had it now.

With bigger and braver bounces she made it all the way to the bottom. The whole group cheered and clapped as she put one shaky foot and then the other on the ground.

Dan unclipped her from the rope and gave her a hug. Noah gave her a hug. A nice long one. She couldn't stop smiling.

"Off belay!" she screamed up to Maureen, and pulled the rope twice.

Away from the group Ama made a jump of pure joy. It was an unprecedented joy, full of opposing properties and opposing parts that for Ama, in that moment, fit together effortlessly: the joy of leaning back, the joy of letting go, the joy of her feet sticking, the joy of pulling them off the rock, the joy of hanging, the joy of not falling, the joy of the past and of the future, the joy of the sky and the mountains and the valley, the joy of having made it, and the joy of not having to do it again.

Jo was woken by the ring of her cell phone at eleven o'clock the next morning.

"Hello?"

"Jo, it's me."

"Who's me?" Jo asked groggily.

"Bryn!" Bryn squawked, as though she was Jo's best friend and it had never been any other way.

The memories of the previous night came back to Jo in stages, starting with the tacos and moving backward.

"You should come over here right away," Bryn said excitedly.

"Where?"

"To the restaurant!"

"Why?"

"Because I think Richard wants to talk to you."

Oh, please. The restaurant suddenly seemed so far away to her. "Bryn, I'm not coming over there. I'm not even at the beach. I'm back home in D.C."

"Can you get back here?"

"No! Bryn, I got fired, remember? Why does Richard want to talk to me?"

"Because he found out what happened."

Jo leaned back on her pillow. She kicked off her covers and crossed one knee over the other. "So what happened?" she asked at the end of a pause.

"Megan saw everything. After you left, Megan told Richard that Effie pushed you into the table and made you smash all that stuff. Carlos said he saw it too."

Jo sat up straight now. This was getting interesting. "Really?"

"Yes. So Effie got fired too. And it was a *lot* uglier with her."

Jo couldn't help enjoying the idea of that. "Really. Whoa."

"Yeah. She got really mad at Megan. She screamed at everyone. Even a couple of customers."

"No way."

"Seriously. You should have seen it. Richard said he was going to call the police if she didn't leave quietly."

Jo shook her head. This was almost too much.

"Unbelievable, right?"

"Unbelievable," Jo concurred.

"Today, we've all been sitting around saying how bad we feel about you getting blamed and everything," Bryn said cheerfully.

Jo realized that Bryn would be on any side of a fight, just so she felt like she was part of the action.

"And also, guess what?"

Jo couldn't guess.

"Zach is here. He's the one who said I should call you."

Jo put the phone down for a moment and squeezed her eyes shut. She picked it back up and put it to her other ear. "Oh, really."

"Yes. He really wants to see you. You should come back, Jo. Seriously. I know it's almost the end of summer, but Richard would probably give you your job back. He said, and I quote, that you were 'a first-rate bus girl.' "

Jo couldn't help laughing. "He said that?"

"Yeah. Everybody feels really bad about what happened. It's so unfair. I said I would tell you that. They totally want to invite you to come out tonight. We would have so much fun."

Jo nodded. She smelled something cooking downstairs. Was it bacon?

"So are you gonna come back?" Bryn asked.

Jo didn't answer at first.

"Come on, Jo. Think how cool it will be. Because then when we start school, you and me, we'll be, like, the cool girls hanging with all these upperclassmen."

That had sounded thrilling to Jo at the beginning of the

summer, but it didn't now. She knew exactly how much Bryn's friendship was worth.

Jo thought she smelled eggs, too. And maybe even toast. She pictured her dad and the mess shaping up in the kitchen. "No," she said to Bryn. "I think I'm going to stay here."

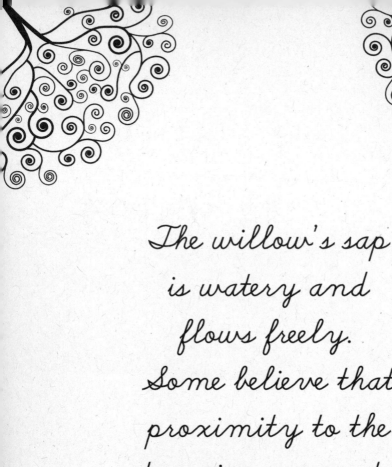

The willow's sap
is watery and
flows freely.
Some believe that
proximity to the
tree gives access to
blocked emotions,
to grief and loss.

Twenty-two

"**Y**ou will spend the first day in wardrobe and fashion, the second day in hair and makeup, the morning of the third day in catwalking and media. The final afternoon you'll put it all together for the competition."

The speaker at the front of the room was a former model named Karen, as thin as a pin in black leather pants. Polly was awed by the length of her legs and the bowed distance between her two thighs. Some of the girls claimed to recognize her from old ads and magazines, but Polly didn't.

Between camp and this place Polly was meeting quite a few former models this summer. Now she knew where models went when they weren't models anymore—to places where they could make more models.

"We'll send each of you down the runway with lights and music and professional photographers snapping your picture. The first seven rows of the audience will be talent scouts from all the agencies, big and small. You'll each get four tickets for parents, relatives, friends. How does that sound?"

There was excited chatter among the audience in the ballroom of the Grand Regent Hotel and some bursts of applause. Polly tipped around on the metal legs of her chair.

A girl in the first row raised her hand and got called on. "How does the competition work?" she asked.

"At the end of the show, each of you will be given a list of the agents and other talent professionals who've requested meetings with you," Karen explained. "Those meetings will take place in ten-minute time slots after the show and the lunch that follows. The model with the most requests will also win a one-thousand-dollar shopping spree, a two-page fashion spread in *GlamGirl* magazine, with a readership of over one point one million girls, and a tryout for *Who Wants to Be a Supermodel?*"

This was met with a hush and then a lot more chatter. Polly too was amazed. Just like that you could turn from a regular kid into a real, professional model with your pictures in a magazine and a tryout for a TV show.

Polly was sent off to Studio B with about twenty-five

other girls. Studio B turned out to be between Studio A and Studio C in another giant meeting room divided by plastic folding partitions. It was lined by long tables covered with clothes and accessories. Each girl was supposed to have a brief turn with a professional stylist. *They use the word* professional *a lot around here,* Polly mused absently.

She sifted through clothes alongside the other girls as she waited for her turn.

"How tall are you?" a tall girl asked to her right.

"Five four," Polly answered. "I'm still growing, though."

The girl nodded. She was at least six inches taller than Polly, as was the girl to Polly's left.

"This might work for you," the girl said, holding up a short blue skirt, "since you're short."

Polly nodded, trying not to look short.

"What's your look?" the girl asked.

"My look?"

"Yeah. What kind of image are you going for?"

Polly tried to keep her teeth well inside her mouth. "I'm not sure," she said. She just wanted to look like a model. She didn't know what her look was supposed to be beyond that. Maybe they'd taught the part about your look on all the shopping trips to the mall she'd missed at camp.

"You should probably lose the bracelet," the girl advised.

Polly looked down at her arm. "Lose it?" she said in disbelief.

"You don't have to *lose it*, but, you know, take it off."

Polly could think of no response. If she had any look at all, it was her bracelet. Dia had gotten it for her. It was from the 1920s and it was the best thing she had.

"I'm Mandy, by the way."

"I'm Polly," Polly said, wanting to shield her bracelet from view. What if the professional stylist also wanted her to lose her most precious possession?

"I think it's your turn," Mandy said, pointing to a woman in black tapping her clipboard.

"What size are you, hon?" the stylist, Jackie, asked after she'd taken down Polly's name and group number.

"I don't know. I — I lost . . . a lot of myself."

"What?"

"No. I mean." Polly was still spooked about her bracelet. She needed to get her bearings. "I mean, I went on a diet. So I'm not sure what size I am."

"Okay." Jackie had no doubt seen her share of skinny girls and weird weight-loss ideas. She studied Polly up and down. "You're a little thing, aren't you? Curvy, though."

"I'm trying to fix that," Polly said.

"What do you mean fix it? Curves are nice."

"Not for a model."

"Not everyone has to be built like a model."

"Models do."

266

Jackie looked at Polly like she thought she was trying to be funny, but she wasn't.

"Do you think I couldn't be a model?" Polly asked seriously.

Jackie let out her breath. "Hon, I'm just here to help you find something to wear."

On the last night, Ama carefully brushed and braided Maureen's hair in front of the campfire. She'd used the last of the Kiehl's to demonstrate to Maureen its magic.

"Okay, let me see." When she had finished, Ama turned Maureen around to admire her work.

"How does it look?" Maureen asked eagerly.

Ama tried to remember how she'd seen Maureen on the first day, but she couldn't. She couldn't conjure any other look than this very nice one in front of her.

Carly was watching the makeover with interest. "Wow. Very cool, M. Wait till you see it."

"Really?" Maureen looked genuinely excited as she touched it carefully with her fingertips. "Did you do it like yours?" she said to Ama.

"Yes."

"Good."

Later in the evening Ama took a walk with Noah. On the way out of the campsite she wondered whether he would hold her hand and on the way back he did. She was jubilant about it at first, but soon her hand began to sweat and she worried that it felt fishy and repellent in his. Even though the moon was full and the stars were in the billions, she couldn't think of anything besides her hand. She had to laugh at herself.

She was relieved when they got back to camp and he dropped her hand before anyone could see. Later, when she was done brushing her teeth, he snuck out from behind some bushes. He kissed her on her minty lips. Just a quick one, before they got caught. He pushed a little scrap of paper into her hand.

She went back to her tent and lay there, wishing she could read the piece of paper. Finally she rummaged in her pack and found her flashlight.

On the front he'd written his phone number and his e-mail address. On the back he'd drawn a little picture of a tree and he'd written their names as though they were carved into the trunk connected by a plus sign. He'd made a little heart around them.

"Do you think I should wear a wig?"

"No, Polly. Your hair will be fine."

Polly tried on a red wig. "This is kind of nice."

"Polly, it's really not . . . you."

That didn't seem a problem to Polly. "I don't mind," she said. She felt prettier when she looked less like herself, but she didn't say that out loud. "I wish I hadn't cut those bangs in the first place."

"Yeah, well. They are a bitch and a half to grow out, aren't they? But we can't worry about that right now."

Genevieve, the makeup and hair professional, was very nice but was getting a little stressed out, Polly decided. The runway show was starting in less than an hour, and she had four more girls to get ready.

Polly tried on a blue wig. She tried on a pink spiky one.

"Polly! You can't rub your eyes when you've got eye makeup on. Okay?"

"Sorry," Polly said. She kept forgetting. She didn't wear eye makeup at home.

"If you want you can go on to the next girl," she said.

"You've still got seven minutes," Genevieve said. "I can do more with your mouth, fix your eyes, redo your—"

"That's okay," Polly said, scooting over to the accessories table. The girls behind her were practically having nervous breakdowns for fear they wouldn't get made up in time.

Polly tried on long strands of fake pearls and chandelier

earrings but decided she should probably not wear them together.

"All right, everybody!" cried Karen, the former model with the leather pants, clapping to get their attention. "Ten minutes! We need to start assembling. If you're in the first group and you're ready, please come to the front of the room."

Polly pinned a brooch to the fabric of her dress just over her clavicle. She wasn't till the third group, so she had time. She checked it in the mirror. Was that how you were supposed to wear these things?

Darn, she'd smeared her lipstick again. She tried to fix it, teetering toward the mirror on her high heels. She knew she had the look of a little kid who'd gotten loose in her mother's dressing room. Not *her* mother's dressing room, because her mother didn't have stuff like that, but Jo's mother's, for example.

She heard a moan from behind her. From behind the table she saw an arm and an elbow and then a head that belonged to Mandy. Mandy's face was red and her sparkly eye makeup was running and refracting in her tears.

"Are you okay?" Polly asked, approaching her by small steps. "What's the matter?"

"My stockings have a huge hole and a run down the back." Mandy's words came out in a sob. She turned around to show Polly.

"Second group, up to the front!" Karen shouted.

"I'm in the second group!" Mandy wailed. She dug her fingers into Polly's arm. "What should I do?"

"Can you get a new pair?" Polly asked.

"No! I tried! There are no other blue ones or gray ones or dark ones. I have to wear dark ones for this outfit."

Polly felt terribly tense about what would happen with Mandy's eye makeup if she kept on crying. She felt tears beginning in her own eyes, partly out of sympathy and partly because Mandy was squeezing her arm so hard.

"Can you go without any?"

"No!" Mandy let out another sob. "Polly, I'm not going to go. I can't. I'm going to tell Karen."

Polly looked down at her own dark legs. "You can have mine," she said quickly.

"What?"

Polly started pulling her stockings off. "These would look good. They're even darker than yours."

"But you need them."

"I think my outfit looks good either way," Polly said, trying to sound confident.

"But you're short."

"They stretch," Polly declared. "That's the thing about them."

"Are you sure?"

"Yes. Go!"

"Third group! Please begin to assemble," called Karen.

Polly could hear the loud music starting from the runway.

"Hurry!"

Mandy pulled and stretched and got the stockings on.

"Lean down," Polly ordered. Mandy did so obediently, and Polly tried to clean up the running makeup with a tissue. Her hands, though inexpert, did a pretty good job. "Okay," she breathed. "Go."

Mandy hugged her and gave her a kiss on the cheek. Polly felt Mandy's tears on her face and the slick of lipstick on her cheek.

"This is supposed to be a competition, girls!" Karen yelled at them. "Let's get going!"

Polly watched Mandy skitter to the end of her line and sent her hopes along with her. She thought, for some reason, of all the slow afternoons of Sunday soccer, rooting for Jo and picking grass on the sidelines. She'd begged her mother to let her play, but she'd never really had the knack for competition.

When Ama's group piled onto the bus the next morning for the drive to the airport, Jared handed out their final reports.

Ama took hers with some trepidation. *It doesn't matter,* she told herself. *You know what you did here. That means more than any grade.*

When she opened it she saw that she'd gotten an A. She almost laughed, as much out of surprise as happiness. It was nice, yes, but it looked slightly flimsier than As usually looked to her, as though it knew it was kind of beside the point.

She went to the back of the bus and sat next to Jared. "I was the worst person on the trip," she said. "Why did you give me an A?"

Jared laughed. "If you're talking about competence, maybe. Not if you're talking about effort."

Ama laughed too.

"Anyway, don't tell this to anyone, but we like to give everybody an A," Jared said in a low voice.

"Really?"

"Yeah. Everybody who finishes."

When they were milling around in the parking lot at the airport, Ama was surprised to see two other buses pulling in filled with two other groups from Wild Adventures. It was like looking at alternate universes.

When the other groups filed out of their buses, Ama was also surprised to see several other black kids. At least three in one group, four in the other.

So she wasn't the only one. Not even close. She felt guilty about all the pictures she'd refused to smile for.

She couldn't resist asking Maureen about it when she came over to help Ama with her gear. "How come they didn't put me in one of those groups?" Ama asked, gesturing toward the two buses parked across the way.

"What do you mean?" Maureen asked.

"I mean when they divided up the groups, why didn't they put me with other black kids?"

"Oh." Maureen shrugged. "I don't know. We don't ask for that information on the application. I didn't know you were black."

Polly tried to walk down the runway in a manner that was strident and seductive, as she'd been taught, but the shoes were very difficult to walk in. Without the dark stockings, she was afraid her short, bias-cut dress looked like a bad figure-skating outfit.

She felt like her skirt was sticking to her bare leg and she wanted to look down and fix it, but she was scared that if she did, she would lose what tenuous grasp she had on her runway walk and pitch into the photographers.

Cameras flashed. Spotlights roved and music blared. The audience was in darkness.

As Polly teetered to the end of the walk and executed her

turn, a spotlight roved over a face she knew. It was Dia. Dia, who'd said she wasn't coming but had come. Dia, who was supposed to be meeting with the people at her art gallery this afternoon.

Suddenly Polly felt like her posture was crumbling. Dia never came to any of her things, but she'd come to this. She was clapping for Polly and Polly had to resist the urge to wave at her. Polly stumbled a little on the way back to the curtain. She was desperate to get to the end of the walk. She was aiming forward, walking too fast, tipping on her heels, not remembering about being seductive or strident. She just wanted this part to be over and to go see Dia.

As soon as Polly got through the curtain and out of the view of the audience, she scrambled through the backstage madness and went out the side door of the ballroom, where the audience was assembled. There was a break before the next group of models and Polly wanted to see Dia, to let her know she knew she had come.

One song ended and it took a few moments of apparent DJ scramble to get another one started. Polly got stuck a few rows behind where Dia was sitting and tried to squeeze past some of the folding chairs to get through. She waved her arms in the hope that Dia would see her.

In the absence of music, Polly heard a familiar voice. It was a gift of Polly's that she never forgot a voice. "I tried to do her makeup," Genevieve was saying to another woman whose voice Polly didn't recognize. "I don't know how much good it did. She's the sweetest kid, but *God knows* where she got the idea she could model."

"She needs braces, obviously," Genevieve's friend said.

Polly froze. She brought her arms down to her sides. The runway was temporarily empty. The music hadn't begun. Polly knew they were talking about her. She started to back away, because she didn't want them to see her there.

Polly saw her mother directly in front of Genevieve, but she no longer felt like getting anybody's attention. She hoped her mother hadn't been paying attention to Genevieve. She hoped she wouldn't turn around. Polly wished that the music would start again and the next model would go and that the conversation would be swallowed up and forgotten in the ensuing noise. Polly would flee backstage and see her mother after the show was over. But it was not to be.

Polly was standing behind some tall people, waiting for her moment to make a run for the side door, when she saw Dia turn around. From the set of Dia's body, the look of her face, Polly sensed there was trouble.

"Excuse me, but what is that supposed to mean?" Dia demanded, glaring at Genevieve. Her voice was angry in a way that cut through the frivolity of the place like a hatchet.

Genevieve stared at Dia in surprise. "I'm sorry. Are you talking to me?"

Polly knew the look on her mother's face. She wished she had stayed backstage. She felt cursed by her combination of soft feet and fine ears. She took a step forward. "Dia, it's fine," she said, forcing her voice up and out. "She didn't mean anything."

Dia barely registered Polly's presence. "Yes, I am talking to you," Dia raged toward Genevieve.

Polly was suddenly afraid Dia was going to shove Genevieve. She took another step toward her mother.

"What I meant was — What I said was —" Genevieve did not know what she was dealing with, and she was too staggered to ask.

"What you said was what?"

Genevieve glanced briefly at Polly. She was mortified, flustered and defensive. "I said she's a sweet kid who maybe isn't cut out to be a model."

The music finally scratched back on, but not loud enough to muffle anything.

"Dia, it's fine. Seriously," Polly whispered. She was shaking.

Dia still had her death glare trained on Genevieve. "And why do you say that?" The contortion of her features made Polly look away.

"She's — she's not tall," Genevieve said haltingly. "She's —"

"She's a *beautiful girl*," Dia cut in, her voice ragged and raw.

Polly put her hands to her face and closed her eyes. When she looked again, she saw her mother's face, no longer angry but desolate.

Twenty-three

Polly didn't want to go back into the audience. So she waited backstage for the lists to be handed out. All the girls were screaming and giggling in groups, reliving the big moments. Polly stood by herself with her hands clasped near her face, trying not to cry.

A lot of them were grouped around the refreshment table, downing bagels and turkey wraps and mini-brownies. Polly wasn't the only girl who hadn't been eating much the last few days. She wanted to feel hungry, but the feeling didn't come.

Karen's three assistants were feverishly working on computers in the office area at the back of the room. Polly heard the huff of the printers going and going.

Mandy came by and hugged her again, but a little more awkwardly this time. "Good job," she said.

Polly just blinked and nodded. She didn't trust herself to open her mouth. She wondered if her mom was waiting for her or if she'd left.

When Polly looked up again Karen was once more clapping and shouting to get the attention of the group. "We haven't done the final tabulation, folks. This is complicated. But we do have some lists to start passing out. When we call your name, please come to the front."

Polly watched the girls who got called dispersing through the crowd, waving their flapping trophies. She caught sight of a couple of the lists. Each showed at least five agents. All the girls were gathering around, wanting to know. One girl's list fluttered by and Polly saw she had at least twenty names.

What if Polly didn't get any? What if she didn't get any paper at all? Would she just go back to her room and pack her suitcase to go home? She tried to gauge her own level of disappointment, but she was preoccupied with thinking about Genevieve and her mom and she couldn't quite discover it.

More girls. More lists. She saw longer ones, shorter ones. One had meetings listed all the way to the bottom of the page and continuing on the back. Would that girl be the one who got the shopping spree and the TV tryout and her pictures in the magazine? Would she be the one whose name was announced as the winner?

What would it be like to be that girl? Polly tried to imagine it, but she stopped, because she couldn't. She wondered if her mother was waiting for her.

When Polly heard her name called, she didn't recognize it at first. It didn't sound like her name in this setting.

"Polly!" Mandy shouted. She gave Polly a thumbs-up.

Polly stumbled to the front. Karen's assistant folded the paper and handed it to her. "Nice work," she said generously.

Polly was suddenly afraid to open it. Had the other girls' sheets been folded? She wished she was half a foot taller than the rest of these girls rather than half a foot shorter so they could all look in. You had more privacy when you were tall. She opened the paper a little and peered in.

There was a name. There was a meeting. There was just one, but there wasn't none.

She held the paper tightly in her hand as she went back to her chair. The paper was damply wrinkled as she opened it again and studied it more closely. She had a meeting with a person named Rod Meyers at 2:10 in Meeting Room 4. Was he an actual agent? Or a talent scout? Did he work for one of the big companies the other girls talked about?

Maybe Genevieve and her friend were wrong. Maybe

Rod Meyers saw something in Polly that Genevieve and the others had missed.

Polly had a meeting. Just one. But one was a number. It was an infinite amount more than none.

Ama surprised herself again by getting teary when she was saying good-bye. Especially with Maureen. Even with Carly. She tried not to show it. She promised Carly she would stay in touch and she really meant it. Now that Ama knew Carly hadn't made out with Noah, Carly's penchant for making out with everyone else didn't seem so problematic.

Noah kissed her, even though everyone could see. She caught Maureen smiling and blushed.

"Write me an e-mail tonight when you get home," Noah whispered. She liked his breath against her ear. It made her shiver.

"I will," she said.

Later, Ama sat on the plane, enjoying the neatness of it, loving the feeling of going home. She sank back into her seat with a sweet exhaustion, thinking about her parents and Bob. She thought of Esi. She kept thinking of Jo and Polly.

Ama looked down at her thighs on the seat, proud of how much stronger and more muscular they were than when she'd started. She examined the delicate ballet flat at the end of each of her legs. She'd been so excited for weeks about putting on her favorite shoes again, but now they struck her as trendy and insufficient.

In wonderment at herself, she stood up and opened her overhead, rummaged around in her pack, and took out her boots. She put them on.

She walked up and down the aisle in her boots. She couldn't sit still. She was burning to talk about Noah. She was burning to tell about her rappel and Carly, and Maureen and the view from the top of the cliff. And Noah.

She had expected she'd want to call Grace as soon as she got back, but it wasn't really Grace she wanted to tell. She pictured Grace's surprise and disapproval at the idea of her having a boyfriend. Grace was pretty judgmental about girls who had boyfriends. "You notice it's the girls with boyfriends who always bomb the bio quizzes," Grace had said to her last year. Ama shook her head. Really it was Polly and Jo she wanted to talk to.

Jo finally reached her mom on her cell phone to tell her she didn't want to go back to the beach house.

"Dad says it's okay if I stay. The summer's almost over anyway."

"What about your job?" her mom asked. She was in the car on her way back from Baltimore.

"It's over."

"It is?"

Jo stood at her bedroom window and watched her father in the backyard pulling weeds from the garden. He was wearing flowered gardening gloves.

Jo didn't feel like holding back from her mother at that moment. "Can I tell you something?"

"Of course."

"I got fired."

"Oh, no."

"Yes. I dropped a tray full of glasses of red wine and cranberry juice on four customers."

"Oh, Jo."

"The glasses shattered and wine went everywhere."

"Oh, no."

"Yep. And one of the customers was a pregnant lady in a white dress."

Her mom made an unexpected sound, and it took Jo a second to recognize that it was a laugh. It was a nice sound.

Jo laughed too. "Not even you could have gotten that dress clean."

Jo decided not to explain that Effie had pushed her or the reason why Effie had pushed her. That was a less funny story for another time.

Their laughter was like a blossom, lovely but short-lived. When it faded the silence stole in.

"Can I tell *you* something?" her mom asked.

"Of course," Jo said.

"I'm going to look at an apartment in the Bethesda Tower on Friday."

"Dad told me that," Jo said.

"Did he?"

"Yeah. He said usually the woman stays in the house and the man moves into an apartment, but that you wanted an apartment and he realized he wanted the house."

"You'll still be with me every other week," her mom said. "We'll be at the new apartment together."

"I know. He said that too."

"It's not permanent. Not at all. But for now I could use something smaller and more manageable. It'll be a lot easier to keep clean."

Jo nodded without saying anything. Out her window she watched her father pouring soil around the azalea bushes and getting a lot of it on his feet. She wondered if he had fired the gardening service, because in spite of his weeding, it all looked quite lush and overgrown.

"And it won't have the . . . memories," her mother said.

Jo pressed her palm against the window glass. "I know," she said. She remembered the week after Finn died, her mother on her knees on the old rug in Finn's room trying to scrub out the stains.

• • •

Polly went up to the hotel room. Her mother wasn't there.

Polly brushed her hair and her teeth. Her ice-skating dress was scratchy and uncomfortable, but she felt like she should keep it on until after the meeting.

At two o'clock she went downstairs and stood outside Meeting Room 4. When it was her turn to go in, her hands were nervous and cold as she reached out to shake with Mr. Meyers.

"And you are . . ." He looked down at his paper.

"Polly," she said. "Polly Winchell."

"Right," he said. "Why don't you sit down?" He gave her a big, very white smile.

"Okay." She sat. Her posture was straight.

"Polly, go ahead and smile for me, would you?" He was leaning forward a bit, looking at her closely.

Self-consciously, Polly smiled a small smile. She thought of what the woman, Genevieve's friend, had said about her teeth. Polly reminded herself that she should not smile big anymore. She should smile small from now on and keep her teeth in her mouth.

"A little more," he said.

Polly didn't want to smile more. It was so unnatural in the circumstance it felt to her like a grimace or a leer.

He nodded. "Polly, I think I could really help you out."

"Really?" she said.

"Yes. Do you know what I do?"

"Aren't you a—"

"I'm a cosmetic orthodontist. One of the best in the business. I've fixed a lot of very famous teeth, a lot of faces you would recognize, but confidentiality prevents me from naming them. Not everybody starts with perfect teeth, right? But there are things we can do. Even in the most difficult cases."

Polly watched his mouth. He had very large, square teeth, and he was saying such unexpected things, she couldn't make sense of them. He worked on people's teeth? He was some kind of an agent who worked on people's teeth? Did that make any sense?

"Are—are you some kind of agent?" she asked.

He laughed. "No, but I do have contacts. Polly, the kind of work I do can make all the difference in getting an agent. That's why I wanted to meet with you." He clicked his pen and began writing. "Polly, I see here you live in—"

"So you aren't an agent at all."

"No."

"You're a dentist."

"An orthodontist."

"Oh."

"One of the best. I'm very well known in my field, as you'll discover if—"

"And you wanted to meet with me because—"

"Because I think I could really help you through ortho-
dontia."

"Because of my overbite?" she asked. Her voice had gotten very quiet.

"Yes. I can see it's a difficult case. It's clear you have an
overbite and a lateral misalignment. That won't work in
front of a camera, of course. You'll need to take care of that
if you want a career."

"And you can take care of it?" she said numbly.

"Yes. I can. It sounds drastic, Polly, but we'll need to
break and reset your jaw. You see, that way we can address
the most serious issues. We can really change the shape of
your face."

Polly sat blinking. She heard with her ears and she
thought with her mind, but she couldn't get the two to go
together.

"Polly, we could have you back here competing next year
to *win*," he said with a confident nod. He considered for a
moment. "Well, realistically, probably more like two years."

Polly stared at him in bewilderment. "You would break
my jaw?"

"I know it sounds —"

Polly stood up. "Thank you," she said.

"Let me give you my card," he said.

"No, thank you," she said.

• • •

288

Luckily the meetings were done for the day in Meeting Room 8. Polly closed the door behind her and sat down in the corner. She put her knees up and rested her head on them. At first she sat quietly and after that she cried. She thought she cried for a long time, but she wasn't sure. There were no clocks or windows in Meeting Room 8.

When she pulled herself together, she navigated the halls back to the lobby and up to the hotel room. Once again, there was no sign of Dia, which was probably just as well.

Polly flopped facedown onto the bed. Her cheek pressed into the thick polyester cover. It reminded her of the texture and pattern of her ice-skating dress. She thought of her mother and Genevieve. She thought of lurching down the runway on her four-inch heels. She felt her tears sinking directly into the bedspread, leaving no evidence they had ever been cried.

Polly let a snuffle out of her nose, but to her surprise it sounded more like a laugh than a cry. She felt her rib cage shaking, and it took her a second to realize it wasn't sobs. She thought of Rod Meyers's teeth. They were funny.

Am I laughing? she wondered. *I think I am.* She laughed until her tears stopped. She reached for a tissue on the bedside table and blew her nose.

She lay down, this time on her back. She looked at the cottage-cheese ceiling and the dead bug in the light fixture. "What was I *thinking*?" she shouted straight upward.

She took a deep breath and sat up. She felt the sense of rising from a dream.

She went into the bathroom and gratefully shed the alien clothes. She quickly showered off the sooty makeup and the hair spray. She watched it all loop down the drain, feeling like she was changing out of a costume she'd worn in a very long play. She put on her soft, plain clothes.

Her vision cleared as she went down in the elevator and walked through the lobby. She had more than an hour before she was supposed to meet Dia and take the train home.

She felt grateful for her flat, comfortable shoes. She wanted to walk. She walked along Forty-fifth Street and turned onto Fifth Avenue. She kept careful track of her turns so she could find her way back.

She saw everything together and nothing in particular. She took in the colorful rush, the multitude of faces, the shiny surfaces of buildings and cars. The sounds wove together into a giant hum in her ears. The world seemed to get bigger and wider as it washed around her. She looked up at the tops of buildings poking at the clouds.

Polly had the strange sensation that she had been living in a tunnel, watching it get dimmer and narrower day by day. And now, suddenly, it was blown open and the world was all around her, just as big as it had always been, and she was part of it again. She had to ask herself, *God, what was I doing in there so long?* She had to ask herself, *How lonely have I been?*

She tried out a thought: she was never going to be a model. Never, never. Even if she did look like her grandmother. She was never going to be tall enough or flat enough. She was never going to be the kind of person who didn't stick out in all directions. To want it was the same as hating herself. That was the truth.

She breathed those words. She could have repeated them a hundred times and they wouldn't have hurt any worse. Reality was stubborn for sure, but it was large and it had possibilities. It was a sweet relief when you let it come.

Twenty-four

In the days since Polly and Dia had returned from New York, Dia hadn't gone to her studio. It was strange for Polly to leave for her first babysitting job of the day with her mother sleeping and come home to have her mother still there, sometimes still sleeping, sometimes watching television, and sometimes just sitting on the screened porch doing nothing.

It was kind of a fantasy at first. Polly had always wished her mother would stay home. She'd dreamed of a mother who made her lunch and wanted to be called Mom. But by the third day of Dia's being home, Polly felt a little spooked by it. Dia wasn't making her lunch or renting movies for them to watch together. She was just lying around.

"Jo called," Dia told her when she got home on the second day. Dia looked uncommonly pleased. It hadn't been lost on her that Jo didn't call much anymore. Dia paid more attention to some things than Polly realized. "She said she's home from the beach. She wants you to call."

Polly wasn't sure. Did Jo really want her to call? And if Polly did call back, which Jo would she get? The Jo who had kicked her to the curb or the Jo who was sorry? Getting discarded by Jo felt bad, but getting the benefit of Jo's guilt didn't feel much better.

On the third day, Polly came home from the Rollinses' in the middle of the day and Dia was lying on the couch. "Ama came by," Dia reported.

"She did? She's home?"

"She just got home. She wants to see you. She looked great."

"Really?" Polly pictured Ama and she felt a pang.

"Yes, go call her."

Polly didn't make a move toward the phone. She was happy to think of Ama, but she didn't want to be disappointed by her.

"Are you okay?" Polly asked Dia.

Dia shrugged. "Just feeling tired," she said.

Polly wanted to ask why she wasn't going to her studio as she'd done roughly every single day for the last fourteen years, but she was afraid to. "I have another babysitting job this afternoon," Polly said. "I have to go in a couple of minutes." Did Dia wish she would stay? Was she lonely? Polly didn't know how to ask.

"Okay," Dia said. She lay on the couch while Polly changed out of the shirt that Nicky had spilled yogurt on and drank a glass of water.

"Call your friends!" Dia shouted after Polly as Polly walked out the door.

It was late by the time Polly returned from the Thomases' house. She was tired from her long day of babysitting, but she'd stopped by Dia's favorite café on the way home and picked up two chocolate éclairs. It was a nice feeling, coming home to someone.

It was dark out, but as she approached the house, she saw that Dia's bedroom light was still on. Maybe they could watch TV together for a while. Maybe they could hunker down under Dia's special chenille blanket and make snide comments about the amateur singers and dancers on the reality shows. Dia had always enjoyed that. "You need to learn how to be more judgmental," Dia had said to Polly the last time they'd watched.

Usually Dia was too tired at night to watch TV with Polly. Usually she came home from the studio and practically passed out on the couch or in bed. But for the past few days it seemed like she'd done almost nothing but sleep. She must have caught up by now.

"Dia?" Polly said as she let herself in the door.

The house was quiet. Polly put her bag down in the front hall. The house looked messy and dusty, more so than usual, even in the dark.

"Hey, Dia?" She wasn't asleep already, was she?

Polly ran upstairs, carrying the bag of éclairs along with her. Her mom loved eating in bed.

"Dia?"

Polly's heart started beating faster before she'd even turned the corner into her mother's room. Why wasn't she answering?

The TV was on, loud. Two candles spluttered on the dresser. The light was on and Dia was sprawled in her chair. There was a glass next to her on the table, a bottle of wine and an empty bottle of vodka tipped over on the carpet.

"Dia?" Polly went over to her mother and prodded her. "Hey. Are you asleep? I brought you chocolate éclairs."

Dia didn't stir. Her jaw was slack and her head rolled back on the chair, but her eyes didn't open. "Hey. Are you okay?"

Polly shook her mother's arm, but nothing happened. "Hey. Dia. Wake up."

Dia didn't wake up. Her eyes didn't even flutter. Polly's heart began to beat harder. Was Dia breathing? Why was her head like that?

"Dia? Dia! Wake up, would you? Hey, it's me! Are you asleep? Why won't you wake up?"

Polly now had both of Dia's arms and she was shaking them hard. Polly's heart was hammering. What was wrong with Dia? Why wasn't she waking up? "Dia, get up! Get up!" Polly heard the crying in her voice. "Please wake up!"

She dropped the bag of éclairs. She put her hands on her mother's face. Was she breathing? She was, wasn't she?

Polly didn't know what to do. Should she call a doctor? Should she call 911? Jo's dad was a doctor. Should she call him? She bolted for the phone, stepping on the éclairs as she went. With shaking fingers she pressed in Jo's number, but nobody answered.

She clutched the phone, needing to do something with it. She called Ama. Ama's parents weren't doctors, but Ama was Ama.

"Hello?"

Polly tried not to sob. "Ama?"

"Polly?"

"Yes," Polly gasped.

"What's wrong? Are you okay?"

"My mom is—she won't wake up. I don't know what to do."

"Oh, my God. Did you call a doctor?"

"No. I tried calling Jo. Her dad—but—" Polly gulped for air. "Should I call nine-one-one?"

"Is she breathing?"

"I think so."

"But she's unconscious?"

"Yes."

"Call nine-one-one," Ama said.

"What if she gets mad?"

"How could she get mad? She's unconscious."

"You're right."

"I'm coming over, okay?"

"Okay."

"Call nine-one-one."

"Okay."

"Polly, you have to hang up first, and then call."

Polly hung up and called 911. She gave them the information and hung up. She sat at her mother's feet and waited.

Polly and Ama and Jo sat in the hospital waiting room together. Ama's dad had gone to get them something to drink. Jo's dad was in the examining room with the ER doctor. He was doing rounds at the hospital that night, so as soon as Jo called him he came down.

Dr. Napoli had come out once already, early on, and told

Polly everything was okay, that Dia could probably go home later that night. He didn't say exactly what the problem was, but Polly had a pretty good idea of it.

An hour or two later, most of the urgency had leaked out of the night, even though the gigantic red emergency cross glowed through the window.

"You don't have to stay," Polly said to Jo and Ama, but they didn't want to go.

Mr. Botsio brought them Sprites and Fritos and went to move the car. Jo and Ama encouraged Polly to eat.

"You are so skinny, Polly," Jo said. "You look like you haven't eaten all summer." Jo's face was not admiring but concerned.

Polly glanced down and tried to like how she looked, but it was harder with them. In their presence, she didn't feel proud of her weight loss. She felt undersized. Both Jo and Ama had grown this summer. Jo was taller and Ama was stronger. Polly suddenly feared she had fallen out of step, gone the wrong way as they surged ahead. Polly suddenly knew she didn't want to stay behind. She wanted to go with them.

While they waited, Jo played songs for Polly on her iPod and Ama drew lines and letters on Polly's back, through her shirt, the way they used to do at sleepovers when they were younger, but she didn't make Polly guess the letters or make words out of them.

Polly felt herself relaxing into the old ways, but at the same time she had the sense that she had come back to them after a long journey. She was the one who'd stayed home this summer, but she wasn't the same girl she had been in June. She'd sensed they had all three changed.

"Hey, Ama, I've been meaning to ask you something." Polly stretched her feet all the way to the chair in front of her.

"Yeah?"

"Why are you still wearing those gigantic boots?"

At last the ER doctor, a woman in her thirties with faded freckles and dark red hair, appeared, followed by Dr. Napoli. Dr. Napoli gave more reassurances and hugged Polly and went back upstairs to his rounds. The ER doctor introduced herself as Dr. Marks and sat down next to Polly in a plastic waiting-room chair. "Your mom is going to be okay."

Polly nodded.

Dr. Marks looked at Jo and Ama, who were perched in the next two chairs. She looked again at Polly. "Can we talk for a minute?"

"Okay."

"These are your friends, right?"

Polly nodded and so did Jo and Ama.

"We can go if you want," Ama offered.

"No, I want them to stay," Polly said.

Dr. Marks pushed up the sleeves of her green hospital smock. "Your mom blacked out because she drank too much. Has that happened before?"

"I could always wake her up before," Polly said.

Dr. Marks nodded. "Do you and your mom live alone?"

Polly nodded.

"Is your dad . . . in the picture?"

Polly shook her head.

"I'm recommending to your mom that she go into an alcohol treatment program for twenty-eight days. There's an excellent facility in Virginia, just about an hour from here."

Polly nodded.

"Is there someone who can stay with you? Or a place you can stay for those four weeks where you'll feel comfortable?"

"Yes." Ama spoke up. "She can stay with me."

"She can stay with me, too," Jo said.

Dr. Marks nodded. "Dr. Napoli mentioned that as well. Good, then." She turned to Polly. Her face was full of sympathy. "Your mom is going to get better, Polly."

"Is she?" Polly asked.

"When she woke up she told me she has a reason, a really important reason, why she has to get better."

"What was that?" Polly asked.

"She said you."

The willow is the
tree of dreaming.

Twenty-five

Jo's eyes felt sore and tired that night, so she took out her contacts and put on her old brown glasses. She'd left her better glasses at the beach.

She brought out her violin from her closet. She opened the case and looked at it, along with her shoulder rest and the little cardboard box with her rosin in it. She touched the fine, smooth wood. She touched a string, but she didn't play.

What would a person like Bryn think of her with her old brown glasses, bowing away on her violin? Bryn would think she was the biggest loser in the universe.

She felt grateful that Ama and Polly always seemed to

appreciate her playing. They used to love it when she played along with the top-ten songs on WKYS. She remembered them dutifully attending her recitals twice a year.

Jo didn't play her violin that night, but she put it under her bed before she went to sleep.

And when she slept, she dreamed of their trees, first as they were in their plastic pots, and then later, when she and Polly and Ama planted them in the woods at the bottom of Pony Hill. She remembered the dirt on her hands, packed under her fingernails.

This was a memory she pushed away in her waking life. Years later, even though she knew the two things were separate, she had begun to conflate the planting of their trees with the dirt and shovel at Finn's burial. But in her dream now, she wasn't afraid of the dirt.

In her dream she pictured the roots of her tree growing under the soil. She saw them winding and circling together with the roots of the trees on either side, Polly's and Ama's trees. She saw them spreading and growing, deeper and wider under all the places she knew, under her house and the middle school and the 7-Eleven and Ama's and Polly's houses. And it seemed to her that there was a whole world under the regular world she knew, and that the roots of her tree connected to all of it, to the foundations of houses and other roots of flowers and shrubs and trees, even communing with the worms and the bugs and other underground things.

And finally her roots traveled all the way to the cemetery and they curled and wound around where Finn was buried and they kept him company under there. Even in her dream she somehow expected that this would be a terrifying image, but it wasn't.

Then the picture in her dream slowly changed and moved up above the ground. Her eyes traveled up to the sky, to the branches and leaves above her, and she suddenly knew that Finn had found company up there too.

The following evening Polly sat in her darkened kitchen with a glass of cold water on the table in front of her. The house was quiet except for her mom upstairs, thumping from suitcase to closet. Dia was packing to go to Virginia the next day. Polly had already packed to go to Ama's, and Mr. Botsio had already stopped by to pick up her suitcase and assure Dia how pleased they were to have Polly stay as long as needed.

Polly sat on the chair with her knees up, her arms wrapped around her legs. She didn't look down when her mom came into the kitchen to survey the contents of the refrigerator. She watched Dia study the bottles of wine and tonic and close the door without taking anything.

"You want a cookie?" Polly asked. Jo had baked three dozen chocolate chip cookies and brought them over wrapped in tinfoil that morning.

"Yes. Thanks."

As Polly watched her mother eat cookies, she didn't feel like she had to observe the bargain of not asking anymore.

"Hey, Dia?"

"Yes."

"Can I ask you something?"

Her mother opened the refrigerator again and got herself a glass of milk. "Okay," she said a little warily. She had a right to be wary.

"Where is all your stuff?"

Her mother gave her a look, wondering if it was worth it to act like she didn't understand. It wasn't. "At the studio, you mean? My work?"

"Yes."

"A lot of the old stuff was sold or packed away."

"And the new stuff?"

Polly's mother put one palm against the steel refrigerator door. She turned her head away.

"You haven't been making any," Polly guessed.

"Not much. Not for a while."

"Why not?"

Dia's face, when it turned back, was sad but not hard. "I lost the idea of being an artist, I think," she said slowly.

"I used to think those trees I made out of the metal junk were clever and beautiful, and the collectors did too. Then I stopped liking them. I tried to make other things, but nobody seems to want anything else from me. My career started to feel like it belonged to someone else."

"Why did you stop liking them?" Polly asked.

Her mother thought about that for a moment. "Because . . . because they seem disrespectful, I guess. To trees."

Polly nodded. She understood. She thought to ask, *Then why do you always go to your studio?* But it would have been a fake question in that she already knew the answer. Her mother would say she went there to find the idea she'd lost. Polly knew that was the real reason, but she also knew that there was a realer reason.

Polly was always wanting her mother, always needing her. She was always wanting one more thing than she got. She was always left disappointed, always wanting, never having. The not having only made the wanting more ravenous and harder to satisfy. She acted like a baby, hoping to get her mother to act like a mother, even though it never worked. Polly knew her mother went to her studio to hide.

"It must be hard for you to understand," her mother said.

Polly nodded. It was and it wasn't.

Her mother turned her face away again. "But try not to

judge me too much until you are older and know more things."

"I'll try," Polly said.

Dia sat down at the table across from her.

"Are you nervous about tomorrow?" Polly asked.

"Yes. And a little bit excited, believe it or not. I am ready for something new."

"I hope it works," Polly said.

"I am really going to try, Pollywog."

Polly nodded. "Hey, Dia?"

"Yeah."

"I need to get braces. I should have gotten them a long time ago."

Dia thought about this. "You're probably right."

"I can go to Jo's orthodontist, I guess, but I don't think I can babysit enough to pay for it."

"You don't have to worry about that."

"I don't?" Polly's mother hadn't sold a sculpture in a long time. Now that she knew the reason, Polly was even more worried about money than before. "Can you afford it?"

"You can."

"No, I can't. I blew it all on that stupid model competition."

"You have a lot of money in the bank," Dia said. She reached over and took a sip of Polly's water.

"What do you mean? What bank?"

"My father was a businessman. You probably didn't know that because I never told you, but he was a big executive at a car company. He died two years ago and he didn't have any other kids and he couldn't stand me, so he left the money to you."

"He left it to me?"

"Yes. The money and a big house in Grosse Pointe, Michigan."

"He left me his house?" Polly was incredulous. "He never even met me."

"He did once. When you were a toddler."

"Really?"

"Yes. He thought you were enchanting. That's the word he used."

"Really?"

"Yes, really."

"Wow."

"I know. He said you were the best thing I ever made. Of course, he was singing a different tune when I was pregnant with you at nineteen and there was no apparent dad around for him to shoot."

"Wow," Polly said again.

Dia rested her chin in her hand. Her cheeks were pink and she looked young to Polly.

"Does it have a pool?"

"What?"

"The house in Michigan."

Dia shook her head, but she looked like she might laugh. "Yes."

"Can I go there?"

"Not with me, you can't. I hate that place," Dia said. "We should really sell it. Maybe that's what we'll do when I get back."

"Why didn't you tell me any of this before?"

Dia shrugged. "It's all pretty heavy. I thought I'd wait until you were older."

"So then why are you telling me now?"

Dia tapped her fingertips against Polly's wrist. "Because you seem . . . older."

Ama was happy to be home. She was happy to eat her mother's food and be hugged and kissed and fussed over.

"We're proud of you," her dad had said to her seriously at breakfast on her first morning back.

"For what?" Ama asked. She hadn't even told them that she'd gotten an A in the course.

"For staying and finishing when you wanted to come home," he'd said.

Ama let Bob sleep in her bed with her the first two nights she was home, just the way Esi used to do for her when she'd first come back from one of her long trips. While Bob lay next to her in the dark Ama told him stories about hiking and climbing and rappelling. She told him how beautiful it was in the mountains and how a river looks from way up high. She even told him about rolling down a hill in her sleep and getting attacked by fire ants and getting lost in the woods for an entire day. But now she told it like it was an adventure, not an ordeal. That was how she would remember it.

"When you get to be in high school," she whispered to her little brother in the dark, "you can't just spend all your time at the library and at school, you know. I'm going to make sure. You're going to go on a wilderness trip like me. You may not love it while it's happening, but I promise you will love it when it's over."

After her mother went back upstairs to finish packing, Polly's eyes wandered to the open pantry and she felt hungry. The light was on in the tiny room, guiding her eyes to the things she used to love and take comfort in—Honey Bunches of Oats, graham crackers, caramel sauce on a teaspoon, eaten straight out of the jar. If you were what you ate, then Polly was still in the pantry.

Polly pictured bits of herself in all the things she would have eaten but hadn't. She was in the cereal boxes, in the bread drawer, in the peanut butter jar, in the refrigerator, floating in the milk carton. In Jo's plate of cookies sitting on the counter.

Polly didn't want to be scattered around the kitchen any-more. She wanted to gather herself back up again. She didn't want to be flat anymore or send herself around the world. She wanted to be with her friends. She wanted to be full.

Twenty-six

Ama woke up in the morning four days before the start of school and looked at the other twin bed in her room. Esi used to sleep there long ago, but for the last few days it had become Polly's. As usual, Polly had woken earlier and had made the bed. She was probably playing with Bob in the kitchen. As glad as Ama and her parents were to have Polly around, nobody was happier than Bob.

Ama was excited because they were going to Staples to shop for school supplies. She was an unrepentant dork in how much she loved school supplies, but it made her feel better that Polly, who wasn't a grade grubber, loved them too. When Ama looked at the calendar, she thought of something else.

She padded into the kitchen in her nightshirt and socks. Polly and Bob were playing Uno. "Do you know what day it is?" Ama asked Polly.

Polly looked up from the cards. "Um. No."

"September first."

Polly understood what it meant. Ama went back to her room to get dressed and Polly came in after she'd finished her card game.

"What do you want to do?" Polly asked.

"Should we call, do you think?"

"We could."

"It's still pretty early," Ama said.

Polly started putting on her socks and shoes and Ama did too. Now that they had thought of it, they couldn't really think about much else.

"We could just go over there," Polly said.

"That's what I was thinking," Ama said.

Jo went to sleep knowing what day she'd wake up into. She woke early and walked to the cemetery. She had avoided it for the last two years, but she was ready to be there now. She sat on the ground, feeling the damp soaking into her pants. She watched the sun rise and point its rays through the trees.

She thought of all the things under the ground, and it didn't scare her as it used to. She was grateful to her dream.

She let a lot of feelings settle over her. Missing Finn. Her parents living separately. The damage she had done to her friendships with Polly and Ama. She was worried these thoughts would crush her if she let them come, but they didn't. You didn't know how heavy they were until you tried to lift them. You didn't know how strong you were.

She would miss Finn forever. That was just the truth, and it was good to know. She decided she would say his name at least once every day and she wouldn't push away thinking of him. Admitting how much she missed him would be a relief. It took a strange kind of energy to keep him away, and she didn't want to try anymore. Maybe she could work on her mom a little.

And as for her parents, it wasn't all bad. She and her dad were finding each other after a long time of being lost. She was hopeful about that. The world had possibilities. Maybe her parents could even figure out how to talk to each other again. You never knew.

The thing that nagged and troubled her was her friends. Polly had been through so much, and Jo had let her down. And Ama. Jo hadn't been awful to Ama, but she had let her drift away.

Sitting together in the emergency room, Jo felt their old promise and it made her hopeful. But so much had happened. Was it too late for them, or could Jo convince them how much their friendship still mattered? Even without special pants or a lame scarf. It was the most important thing she had learned this summer, and she wished she knew how to explain it. What if they had drifted so far that they'd lost the feeling? Could she show them the way to find it again?

Jo felt a light breeze over her shoulders and it lessened her load. She lay on the ground, curled on her side, and put her ear to the grass. She imagined she could hear the roots of the trees growing and reaching.

She must have fallen asleep, because when she opened her eyes, she wasn't alone anymore. She was momentarily so startled, she lost track of where she was and what was happening. She sat up. Ama and Polly were there as though she had summoned them right out of the air.

But it wasn't the air, it was really them. They were both holding pictures that they'd brought. Ama showed her the photograph of the three of them with Finn the year he'd dressed them up as Ewoks for Halloween and gone as Han Solo. Jo was amazed by Polly's drawing of a tree with roots and branches as delicate and elaborate as a spider's web. They laid their offerings carefully against Finn's headstone.

They sat down next to her, one on either side. Polly touched her hand.

Jo put her head down on her arms and cried. They'd remembered. She hadn't needed to tell them or ask.

Ama put her arm around Jo's shoulder. Polly patted her hair. Jo felt safe to cry with them.

Jo hadn't needed to show them the way. Once again, they had shown it to her.

They traced the familiar steps across East-West Highway toward the 7-Eleven. They didn't need to talk about where they were going. They strode arm in arm, which gave Ama a dorky kind of pleasure.

They strutted into the 7-Eleven so much bigger than they'd been before, with their adventures and their disappointments and their big ideas. But they still bought blue Slurpees and candy bars.

They followed their younger, smaller footsteps to Pony Hill and ran down it, losing their footing at the bottom and stumbling forward in their old way.

They stepped into the woods slowly. Ama felt like she was holding her breath. She felt like they all were.

It had been more than two years. She was scared of what they might see. Had the trees withered? Had they died, with no one to talk to them or water them or pour plant food on them or play violin to them? It felt unbearable to Ama, the fear and suspense as they stepped deeper into the shade.

There were no small trees. They looked in the place they

thought their trees should be and saw nothing they recognized. Where were the trees?

"Look at these," Polly said.

"Those couldn't be ours," Jo breathed. "They're so big."

"But look," Polly said.

They looked and saw how the trunks lined up unmistakably, three in a row.

Ama approached them carefully, in awe. She touched a finger to the familiar bark she'd known in miniature. "It's true. These are them. They're willows. Look at the leaves. I'm sure of it." Ama had always done her homework more carefully than the others.

Ama stepped back, a sense of wonder overtaking her. Jo and Polly stepped back too. For a long time they looked up at the canopy of feathery gray-green leaves making a roof over their heads.

It was remarkable to Ama, how the three trees had grown together, intertwining their branches and leaves above. She imagined the roots in mirror image below, mingling under the ground. They were three together, but they were also part of the larger forest now.

The trees were strong. They wanted to grow. They just grew and grew, even when no one was paying attention.

As the three of them walked home from the trees, nobody needed to say it, but Ama knew. They had questioned

their friendship. They had searched and wondered, looking for a sign. And all along they'd had their trees.

You couldn't wear them. You couldn't pass them around.
They offered no fashion advantage. But they had roots.
They lived.

No matter
how far back you cut
a willow tree,
it will
never really die.

Ann Brashares lives in New York City with her husband and their three children. She is the author of the Sisterhood of the Traveling Pants novels, a series that reached #1 on the *New York Times* bestseller list and inspired two major motion pictures. Visit her at www.annbrashares.net.